Just Imagine

Best to you,

Angela

Just Imagine

by Tony Seton

Monterey, California
August 2011

This book is a work of fiction. There is no correlation to real people or events. It is solely the product of the imagination of the author, often stimulated during his daily perambulation in close proximity to the Pacific Ocean, and further nurtured and massaged at the keyboard.

Just Imagine

ISBN-10: 1463676670
ISBN-13: 978-1463676674

Printed in the United States of America

Table of Contents

Acknowledgments. iii

Introduction. v

Preface. ix

Heaven Can't Wait. 1

Down to Earth. 13

Homework. 21

The Guide. 27

The Morning After. 38

Where Do We Start. 48

Piece o' Cake. 55

A Moment's Paws. 63

PSR. 81

Twixt Heaven and Earth. 91

Winging North. 101

The Professor. 110

The Hero Dawg. 123

A Word with the Wise. 135

Who's Calling. 146

All the Time in the World. 157

Epilogue. 170

Author. 173

Acknowledgments

My deepest thanks go to have all who have shown the courage to the push the envelope of their thinking, and through knowledge, to reach for wisdom.

This book is dedicated to Denise Swenson, who provided inspiration, and who also proofread and polished this book into proper shape. She's a magnificent human being.

Introduction

When Jason and Carole asked me to write this book, I said yes – obviously – but I had some reservations. I understood their reason for not wanting to become public figures in a situation like this. There are all too many crazy people in this world looking for ways to show it. And since I was already working with Professor Desmond Hicksaint, the renowned physicist, on his studies of what he named Parallel Spectrographic Recoloration (PSR), I was aware the importance of auras.

Being a journalist first, my concern was that the story Carole and Jason wanted me to tell might trivialize The Professor's work, but after several long conversations with him I realized that Jason's description of auras would reach many right-brained people who would not grok the physics of PSR.

Another concern that I had was how to write their story. It sounded incredible in some places, like how they met, and certainly what had happened to Jason "upstairs", but on the other hand, it was truly incredible. And for that matter, only incredible people were going to realize the truth of it.

Still, since I was changing their names and other references that might have identified them, I didn't want to put out the book as nonfiction because it might be attacked on its face so I'm defining it as non-nonfiction and the critics can have it anyway they want.

In case it matters, I don't believe in a white-bearded white-robed god dispensing iconic justice, but I'm quite clear that there is some force in existence in the universe that is running things. I believe that it becomes visible to us as we increase our consciousness, and that it will become more obvious in the coming years.

People who have beliefs in gods will eventually evolve to a point where they shift their thinking from an external notion of deity to the godhood that is within each of us. Instead of listening to the drone of preachers, they will hold the Christ Consciousness in their own hearts.

So this book is certainly not for everyone...not yet. Nor will the readership be based solely on intellect although the book is likely to appeal to more thoughtful people. The reason is that auras are about consciousness, and consciousness is different from book-larnin'. It has to do with an open mind and an open heart. Indeed, many people we would think of as successful are not as aware as those with fewer degrees or less money.

Consciousness is a quality of the expanded human mind. Though it has always been with us, it only caught on in a big way recently among a growing segment of the population. Back in primitive times, the most conscious person in the clan or tribe was often the shaman or the witch doctor. Later they became the important philosophers. They also were likely the witches in Europe – and in Salem, Massachusetts – who were slaughtered by those who felt their own crude physical power being challenged.

Auras enable us to recognize the level of peoples's consciousness. As you will see in the following pages, the implications of such sight, as it were, are transformative on the level of the fish climbing out onto land.

The ability to see auras will greatly divide the people on this Earth between those who are of lower consciousness and willing to stay down there – usually in fear or anger – and those who are habitually seeking to expand their awareness. It is my guess that when it comes to thinning the human herd, as we might expect will happen in the not too distant future, it will be on the basis of consciousness.

I have no idea how that will happen, but surely we will want the greatest minds on our planet, say the top two billion, to be the ones to build a new global community and all that that entails.

No one is precluded from the future. Understand that anyone can see auras, but first they have to remove a lens cover that was installed in their minds as children. It requires awareness of the cover, and then an exercise of our powers of imagination to spark the dissolution of the lens cover that has been blocking our vision for many millennia.

It can take a little time for that cover to dissolve. It depends on the emotional state of the individual, the quality of their character, and the level of their awareness as they approach the task. At first the sight of auras may appear hazily translucent, but over time, maybe hours or days, the quality of the vision will increase to a new normal.

Just Imagine that you can see auras and soon you will be able to. It's not a belief, it's a deliberate restoration of the lens function.

(Yes, Carole, and it is a good name for a book.)

So sit back, buckle up behind your literary seatbelt, and dive in. You might think that *Just Imagine* is just a more esoteric version of what-if, but there is more. This book also invites people to not only engage the concept, but also to participate – to act – rather than stand outside and ponder what-if.

Tony Seton
Monterey, California
August 2011

Preface

On Jason Isaac's 43rd birthday, he made a delicious dinner for eight of his wife Ellie's friends at their Park Ridge, Illinois home. There were only nine chairs so he ate his dinner standing at the counter in the kitchen overlooking the dining table. He didn't mind. The moving truck would be picking up his things in ten days for his return to California. He didn't even mind when Ellie brought out the birthday cake she'd ordered for him. It had seven candles on it – four and three; get it? – and an inscription that read "Happy Birthday, Dickhead."

Jason thought it was maybe a tad over the top, but the guests all thought it was very funny. One of them used the term "clever" and that certainly was over the top.

But Jason wasn't on MSNBC to begin with. In fact he wasn't employed, at least not at the moment. He was an independent, a freelancer, a person without a financial security blanket. But he was getting out of Chicago after three years, two months and eighteen days, leaving a woman he was no longer in love with, and returning to California. He could handle the appellation.

The drive up into Minnesota and then west across Route 90 was a deliciously cathartic experience. He was rebirthing, in a good sense. From the road he called an old friend who was richer that god who had a house in Livingston, Montana, that was never used. His friend told Jason that he was welcome to stay there on his way...on his way home. It was a huge house, nestled in a bend of the Yellowstone River, with the Rockies across the way, fully furnished, but empty of people. He had his choice of six bedroom suites.

The next morning – this was the third week in September – he woke up at seven and the sun was climbing over some lower peaks. The thermometer outside read 21 degrees, but without so much as a breeze, it didn't feel cold at all as Jason walked out to the river, his camera around his neck. Mist was rising from the warmer water into the colder air. Less interested in that phenomenon than they were in Jason, who had suddenly appeared on the scene before them, were two huge elk. Not sure how they felt about their pictures being taken, Jason smiled weakly and backed out of range.

He might have stayed for days or a week or more, except that this was Thursday morning and the movers were going to arrive in Mill Valley at ten on Monday morning, and they were wondering where they were to meet him to unload his furniture. Jason didn't know where that was either - he presumed he could find some place over the weekend; he'd always had great good luck finding places to live - but it meant he couldn't dawdle. Still, he made a side trip to Yellowstone Park, viewed the bison, Old Faithful, and visually arresting steaming hot springs in colors that might have stumped Disney.

Jason arrived at a friend's house in San Rafael at five on Friday. On Saturday morning, after a check of the newspaper – these were pre-Internet days – he found himself checking out an apartment in Tiburon that he was to live in for the next year and a half. It was a beautiful spot with a wall of glass that looked south and west toward San Francisco and Sausalito. He would regularly enjoy the sight of the fog fingering its way down the Bay side of the coastal ranges. It was another display of nature's magic.

After five years of futzing around with good-paying but infrequent freelance gigs, and a variety of relationships that promised equally little future, he decided it was time to head south. No, not that far. He'd been to LaLa a dozen times and it never captured his imagination. If you can't imagine doing well or being happy in a place, it's not the place for you.

South for Jason was an offer from a communications firm that specialized in high-tech roll-outs and Republican politics. They were located in Monterey, which Jason loved. They had chosen the spot because there was little high-tech – that was all up north in SillyCon Valley – but there were plenty of wealthy Republicans willing to sign checks. Ironically perhaps, the firm couldn't find decent local candidates in whom to invest, except at the Christian school board level, but state and national candidates were glad to take up the contributory slack.

Unfortunately for Jason, when the firm went belly-up he was again trying to find sources of income. An ex-brother-in-law told him to woo the Pebble Beach divorcees looking for boy candy. Jason wouldn't admit it but his thoughts had visited that script but found that it required the same postured smile of political candidates or Los Angelenos, something he couldn't pull off while sober for more than a few minutes.

Then one day when the mailbox was choking on all of the bills and he felt like he couldn't even count on the sun to rise in the East the next morning, Jason got a call from a woman who had worked in the next office at the now-defunct communications company. Cindy Bevelaqua was a graphics person with a quiet demeanor and considerable design talent, usually above what clients would understand let alone appreciate. She would briefly try to explain the concept behind her work, which Jason always thought made sense, but then she would be stopped when the bill-payers gave her that doesn't-work-for-me grimace. Then she would take out something she had knocked off without inspiration, and they would be wow'd. No one said that life is fair.

Cindy thought equally highly of Jason's ability to write. She had been downright surprised at the speed with which he was able to turn out copy, which he attributed to his broadcast news background. He had described it to her as "Type, don't think." That's why she had called. There was a retired industrialist in Pebble Beach who'd had an interesting life, starting with his being the 18-year-old skipper of a PT boat that made raids against the Japanese among the many islands of the Philippines.

"The guy thinks he doesn't have a lot of time left. He's only 73, but he's still carrying shrapnel," she explained to Jason, "So he wants to get his memoir written for his grand-children. I got this from his niece who I sometimes go riding with. Is that something you could do? I could do the cover for him."

Bang-zoom, and Jason was off on a new career of writing biographies for rich people. He didn't take the work lightly, especially because everyone he spoke with had an interesting story, even if it took some prodding for them to reveal their truths. It took about two months to get the text and inside images together. Meanwhile, Cindy took care of the photography and illustrations.

They were able to produce four books a year without serious effort, when two would have covered his expenses and then some. And because of the area they were in, when one person came out with a biography, there were others who decided it was necessary to have their book done. Concerned that it appear like a fad, Jason limited the number of clients and had a waiting list that would keep him comfortably occupied for as long as he needed to eat and live under a roof.

Maybe life got too easy for Jason. He was visible and popular in the social scene, often photographed with his famous clients at this event or that which were very often benefits for the myriad causes that were forever trying to suck funding out of the community. And in that frequent mingling, Jason found himself quite popular with the single women – the widows and yes, the divorcees. He was one of the few unattached men under sixty who wasn't on a string, so he could be quite selective with those for whom he might play the consort at an evening of cheap caviar, trite music, and boring speeches that combined endless thank-you's and guilt-edged begging.

Jason enjoyed the flirting and luxurious surroundings of the follow-up. He didn't choose his partners on the basis of their wealth but the fact that they were attractive, and not just physically. He wasn't a wham-bam-thank-you-ma'am kind of guy. He wanted someone with whom he could have an intelligent conversation. Stimulation sitting up, as he referred to it.

A few relationships blossomed though they were mostly based on amity rather than sex. Since he could remember, his sexual interest in women seemed to peter out, as it were, after the first or first several encounters. He made the analogy was that he was like a dog who was incessantly sniffing other dogs. He didn't know why, he would readily admit, and there were times when – big sigh – he wished it were otherwise. That he could settle down for a long-term relationship with one woman whom he adored and whom he wanted sexually forever. But she never appeared on his stage, at least not in this first half of his adult life.

Plus he was truly enjoying himself. He ate well, drank ridiculously expensive wines, and was showered with gifts; tokens of appreciative involvement. Sometimes he received larger gifts as lures for repeat performances, but he tended not to accept them. He didn't want to get a reputation as a gigolo, or even a slut, so he always gracious and friendly, and very discreet. Not all of the women were similarly-minded, of course. Many of them even compared notes, which served not their individual interests but to increase the mystery about Jason, and concomitantly, his desirability.

Life was good in that at last he was having all of the women he wanted, and he controlled the flow of his revenue stream. And he'd accomplished all of this without being a dickhead; at least in his own mind. His ex-brother-in-law, whose voice dripped with jealousy, told Jason that what he was looking for love...not in all the wrong places, but with his wrong head.

"You'll never find the right woman that way," he insisted, and Jason knew that he cared, but...

"I'm not looking, Danny," Jason insisted right back. "And besides, you never find what you're looking for if you're trying to find it. Only if you're not looking. That's when you know you've found the real thing."

Then Jason hung up on the him, after sending his truly warm regards to his ex-wife who had left him because their sex life had evaporated, along with their savings.

Jason's subsequent conversation with himself revolved around the fact that having as much fun as he was – and giving as much pleasure as he always and generously did, for the duration – was a grand thing. He loved the falling in love – or at least in like – with a new woman. The discovery was ambrosia. Anything goes. And real Champagne. It was all much better than his past life.

What more could he want? To love, he admitted to himself while lying awake in the middle of the night. But alas, as Mick Jaggar pointed out,"You can't always get what you want, but if you try sometimes, well, you just might find, you get what you need."

But in daylight, Jason told himself that he didn't need anything, thank you, Danny, and he dismissed the man's attempt to unsettle his swimmingly fine lifestyle.

Like his opinion mattered...not. It turned out that it wasn't what he wanted or needed, but that he was needed.

Heaven Can't Wait

Jason Isaac stood expectantly as if waiting for the doors of an elevator in which he was riding to open. All around him was blackness, but there was no feeling of fear. No problem, maybe. Then the blackness parted and he found himself standing in a large reasonably appointed lounge area. The place looked like an upscale version of the Red Carpet club at the Minneapolis-St. Paul airport on Larry Craig Loyalty Day, but more gracious than fay.

There were maybe twenty separate enclaves over an area the size of a gymnasium. Recessed lighting, light pastels, and a lot of glass and chrome that could have been picked up for a song at an institutional estate sale. Directly across from Jason in a small, private area there were three people sitting in comfortable deep leather lounge chairs. They were all looking toward him, and one, an older man who reminded Jason of Michael Rennie twenty years after Gort rescued him (*The Day the Earth Stood Still*, 1951), was beckoning him with a kind face and several fingers.

Jason checked out the other two as he walked toward them. One was a rather attractive brunette, maybe in her late

1

thirties who might have been Beaver Cleaver's teacher, Miss Landers. The third person was a sorta intimidating-looking somewhat older and definitely colder woman, with an albino skin tone, blood red lipstick and a Sinead O'Connor hair cut, right down to the skull. It turned out her name was Sinead. The brunette was SueLan, and the older fellow called himself Klaatu.

"Welcome ," said the smiling Klaatu as the three of them stood for him. SueLan was smiling, too, but Sinead's expression could have chilled Margarita glasses. "We're glad you're here, Jason. I trust you had a quiet transition."

Jason, feeling instantly confident, said,"Well, yeah, you know I was, getting some relief after a stressful day. And then poof, here I am...." He thought for a moment. "I think I kinda left matters unresolved, if you know what I mean."

They shared a glance amongst themselves and then looked to him again.

"Yes," said Klaatu thoughtfully,"I imagine you might have heard a scream as you were leaving, is that right?"

"Yes," Jason corroborated. "That was Mimi. She thought I was dead."

"A good reason to scream, ya think?" This from a barely-restrained Sinead.

Jason gave her a look and sidestepped her question. "Um, I'm used to happier screams, myself."

"That's my sister down there," Sinead informed him, punctuating her statement with a snort.

Klaatu gestured for Sinead to calm herself and explained that Sinead had been a cougar a couple of lifetimes ago.

"She looks the type who would pick up young boys," Jason said, and added sarcastically,"and put them on the grill."

2

Klaatu chuckled. "No, not that kind of cougar. The large cat."

Jason raised his eyebrows,"Maybe you want to re-visit your policy on pets here."

Sinead growled.

Jason took a deep breath and took stock of his surroundings. The three people he was sitting with looked like regular people, as previously described, but maybe a little gauzy. The effect might have been accentuated by the lighting in the room, and the fact that they were wearing white toga-like gowns with golden cord belts. There were also several gold chevrons on their cuffs, though nothing ostentatious; SueLan and Sinead each had one stripe while Klaatu had four.

"So I'm guessing I'm dead?" he offered. "This is some kind of *Heaven Can Wait* thing, isn't it?"

"Something like that, yes," Klaatu told him.

"So I'm going back?"

"Yes indeed."

"Will I remember being here, like in the movie?"

The three looked at each other. Klaatu spoke again. "We're not sure. Maybe at the beginning of your return, but then it would get in your way. That's been our experience."

"You do this a lot?"

"Oh yes, quite frequently."

"So this is some cosmic chess game you're playing up here?"

Klaatu gave his version of a scowl; it was quite benign. "No, no, we're quite serious. We've spent the last 65 years in earnest efforts trying to avoid a full-scale retooling of the Earth. Switching people in and out, trying to change things, in a minimalist way, of course."

"Using dead people whom you rejuvenate?"

Klaatu explained. "Perhaps you might say that, although it's a temporary phenomenon."

"How temporary? I mean, Mimi isn't the sort to go in for necrophilia."

Jason didn't look over at Sinead, thinking he might break out laughing, and he certainly didn't want to get into a cat fight with her.

Klaatu smiled patiently at him; he seemed not entirely unbemused. "You won't be gone that long, not from her perspective. We'll have you back before you're missed."

"Okay, but I can't remember the last time a woman I was in bed with made the mistake of thinking I was dead."

"Trust me," he said in such a smooth voice, Jason immediately gave in. "Time is very different once you, uh, leave Earth." He adopted the tone of a patient eight-grade science teacher. "You see, time is pie-slice shaped. On Earth, where there are only three dimensions apparent to most people, the time you'll be...gone...is just a fraction of a moment. Not noticeable. Like a 100th frame of film. But in the fifth dimension, where we are now, that moment is infinite, as it is in the higher dimensions, where there is even less time."

"I was following you pretty well until that last bit, but I think I understand what I need to. We can jaw for as long as we want and I won't be missed."

"That's right," said Klaatu. Then the science teacher admitted,"There is, however, a minor concern that there might be some leakage. We haven't figured that out yet. It's like a still frame shuttering." He smiled as if to conclude that issue.

"Okay, so I'm not dead," Jason said, noting a look of disappointment on the two women's faces, albeit for different reasons. SueLan was more attractive by the moment. "I'm on a mini-sabbatical."

Klaatu smiled his acknowledgment.

"So, why am I here?"

"Yes, exactly," Klaatu said, beaming at his two lounge mates. "Your acute journalistic mind; that is the reason that you are here."

"Thank you, I think."

"Yes, here's the situation. SueLan?"

SueLan grabbed the proverbial ball and ran with it. "You see, here's the problem. You're species has gotten stuck, and that has put the Earth at risk. Well, not really. The Earth will always survive, but we don't want to wait a half-million of your years it would take to clean up the mess you've made, and seem intent on worsening. We'd rather you take responsibility and restore the Earth to its national beauty."

"I'm with you, sister. It's a mess. Five billion people overpopulated, pollution destroying the environment, every government on the planet in the pockets of special interests, and both the NFL and NBA on lock-out." Jason winked at SueLan. "Actually, I don't give a hoot about professional sports anymore. Not since I interviewed George Steinbrenner. They're all just a bunch of over-paid greedy SOBs who distract people from what's really important."

SueLan looked glowingly at Jason. Then to Klaatu, exuberantly, "I think he was a good choice." Jason had that effect on women.

"So, like what's happening now, here?" Jason asked. "I thought I was supposed to help to change the world through communications. That's what I was told in that first year I was in California...by a psychic, an astrologer, and a palm reader. I was pretty convinced I had some important contribution to make, you know. That sounded big to me." Jason frowned. "But now I feel like I've been coasting that last five years. Getting it done, but hardly saving the world." He looked at Klaatu,"Is that why I'm here, now? To get a new assignment or something."

"Very intuitive, young man," the older man said. "Yes, that's why you are here."

Jason smiled, somewhat self-satisfied but not over doing it. "So what's the gig, then?"

SueLan continued,"You were right when you thought you were going to help to change the Earth through communications. You are needed now more than ever. You have to shift the thinking on your planet, and especially with your American people, since they are the world leaders."

"Moi? And we're talking about a country where millions of people think Bachmann or Palin would do a better job than Obama." Jason sighed. "I was never a big fan of his, and he's one of the biggest disappointments I've seen in 45 years of watching American politics." He peered at SueLan. "Sorry, I was on my soapbox. I detect a note of urgency. Whassup? And why me?"

SueLan looked to Klaatu who picked up the story. "The population is a bomb. There are many too many people on your planet, as you noted. The problem is not only pollution, which has poisoned the atmosphere. It will take you thirty years to make your planet healthy again, once you stop polluting it."

"It's not likely then that I'm going to be around for that then."

"No, not likely, but you will get the ball rolling."

"You sound like you have a lot of confidence in me."

Klaatu smiled at Jason. "We've been watching you for a long time," he said, "in our time terms."

"Ahso," Jason said without understanding, but knowing he didn't need to.

"The over-population has created what you refer to as a too-many-rats-in-a-box syndrome. There are too many people. Their mass of individual energies has created a chaotic situation on the surface of the Earth that has created a distinct wobble in the planet."

"I've heard nothing about that, and I read a lot of different news sources."

"There have been some pieces published in scientific journals, but they have mostly been discounted."

"By the scientists who are in the pockets of the mega-corporations that don't want to disrupt the status quo."

"That's right, Jason."

Jason laughed, but the serious expressions on the faces of SueLan and Klaatu, and the hostility painting Sinead's visage brought him up short. He felt combative."And you think I can do something about this? One person. An uninspired contract writer in Monterey who spends two hours a day just walking on the beach? Am I dreaming or are you?"

Klaatu shook his head. "We appreciate your humility, but we have the right man." He looked to the other two. SueLan nodded affirmatively, Sinead grudgingly.

"But why me? Why not a wised-up Billy Graham, or Tammy Faye without the tattooed make-up? Someone with personality."

Klaatu shook his head again. "No, Jason, you're the one. You have the journalistic credentials and your style --"

"Such as it is," Sinead put in. Jason stuck his tongue out at her quickly. "See what I mean?" she said, helplessly.

SueLan giggled.

Klaatu smiled. "That exactly why you are the one, Jason. You are thoroughly irreverent. You can get people's attention and they will listen, at least to hear what you say, and that's when you have them. Not for long, but you are a very persuasive communicator. You will find your stroke."

Jason succeeded in suppressing even a smile. "What do you want them to be told? What we've talked about? That'll never happen. They are either complete idiots, or they're in denial, most of them. Good grief, the average American household had the television on for 160 hours a month."

Before he could earn an answer, he asked, "And what's the response you expect? Suddenly they all see the light, shove their parents onto an ice floe? There ain't no ice. It's all melted."

He was on a reporter's roll. "And what's your time table? I'm supposed to get this all done during half-time of the SuperBowl? Can I take off my shirt?"

Jason was clearly distressed with the whole idea. "Just how do you expect this message to be delivered?"

"Ach, Mr. Issac," said Sinead. "Are we supposed to do everything for you?"

Jason looked at her quizzically. "Does she have a German accent, or what? She reminds me of Dr. Strangelove. You weren't Eva Braun were you?"

She hissed at him.

8

Jason dismissed her with a scornful look and then sank into himself. They let him be. In a minute he was back with a softer tone. "Do I get any props? You know, like proof that I've been here, or that my story isn't a fake?"

Klaatu exchanged a pleased looked with the other two. "You will be able to see auras when you get back."

SueLan was excited. "Do you understand what that means?" She didn't wait for him to respond. "You know about Kirlian photography where there is an image of a person's unique energy field. " She stopped just long enough to see his nod of agreement. "You will be able to see their aura."

"And?" asked Jason.

"My dear," Klaatu said to SueLan,"Tell him about the book."

"Oh of course, how silly of me, yes." She blushed slightly at her oversight. "There is a new video coming out by another California writer, Tony Seton, about PSR, or Parallel Spectographic Recoloration. It's about a physicist who has written a computer program that reads people's auras. The aura shows a person's level of consciousness, how bright they are, and the degree of their integrity."

"So you can see if a person is just morally sound or if they also have an intellectual basis for being moral. " Jason's eyebrows rose. "That's serious." Then he asked,"Is this for real? What he's doing, this guy? Is the video right?"

Klaatu appreciated his questions. "The video is right on. It features the scientist who wrote the program to see auras. It tells the truth, and in terms that most people can understand. At least those who have reached a certain level of consciousness. He thought of producing a fictional program, since it's easier to engage people with a movie than with a documentary, but the scientist insisted that it be accurate."

It was Jason's turn to smile. "That's right. Very good." His eyes showed some sparkle. "So you're saying I'll be able to see those auras now? On Earthlings, as it were? The live ones."

"That's right," put in SueLan, pleased with their progress. And then anticipating his question,"It will be very clear when you see people if they are honest, if they are aware. In fact you will have to probably restrain your response when you meet people from what you see. There will be some surprises at first, especially people who don't seem very conscious, but then you will find out that they are."

"And vice versa," added Sinead.

"Maybe I'll meet this Seton fellow," Jason mused.

"That California is a big state," Sinead observed unnecessarily.

Jason gave her a long patient smile. "I knew that," he said quietly. Then his face brightened further. "Maybe we should break for lunch?"

His three hosts looked at each other. "You can't be hungry," Klaatu said gently.

"Why not?" Jason asked.

"We don't eat up here," he explained.

"There's nothing to feed on?" Jason asked. "No body that needs nourishment?"

SueLan jumped in. "We're just holograms. Energy beings."

Jason pursed his lips as he opened his hands and stared at them. Then he returned his hands to his lap. "That explains why you didn't offer me coffee," he said with a wan smile, not sure that he liked the situation. Then he added,"I guess I'm not really hungry then. It was probably a social thing, instead of a desire to eat.

"What about help? Will there be others down there who know about this trip?" he asked.

Klaatu answered him, "You will have help, but she won't know about where you've been. You'll have to explain it to her."

"So I'll have my memory of this for a while?"

"For a while."

"What's her name, so I will know her?"

Klaatu shook his head. "No, you will know her."

Jason thought for a while. Then he rose to his feet and walked up to each of them, taking the folder that each had in their laps out of their laps – they offered no resistance – reading the covers and opening them, only to discover that they were empty. When he had checked them all he said, without a great deal of opprobrium, "Hey, no wonder she's on my case." He was looking at Sinead. "She has the wrong folder. Hers is for Issac with two esses instead of two ayes. You and SueLan," he said to Klaatu, "have the right one. Who's that, Sinead? Issac Delgado, the Cuban salsa performer? I didn't know he was dead."

"It's you," Sinead shot back. "No one could mistake you. It's just a typo."

"A typo?" Jason asked, adding an edge to his voice. "What other mistakes are you making?" He let that hang for a moment but he clearly held the floor. "Maybe you shouldn't even have grabbed me," he suggested pointedly. Then his posture changed, and he told them, "No, I know you're right. You have the right person. I don't know how it's gonna get done, but I suppose I'll figure out a way. Or it won't matter, will it?"

Klaatu was on the verge of joy; at least great relief. SueLan was beaming. Sinead was Sinead. It had been a long time since she'd been happy, but she seemed content with her unhappiness.

Jason couldn't resist. "So what happens next? Are you putting me back under Mimi now?"

"I wish you didn't talk like that," his target said

"Shall I say 'hi' for you when I get back?" Without waiting for a response, he looked over at Klaatu. "There's a lot on my plate, and I suppose I should get started. Is there anything else you have for me?"

Klaatu shook his head slowly, "No my boy. Only godspeed."

"Good one," Jason said with a laugh.

Klaatu nodded his head lightly.

They were distracted by a raised voice in another conversation area. There was a gaunt bearded man wearing a long robe that looked like it must have once been quite regal. He had both arms upraised in a gesture of unrequited demand. Jason couldn't see to whom the man was talking, but something in the back of his mind said he should know who it was who was doing the ranting. He turned to Klaatu. "Do we know who that is?"

Klaatu sighed, "Yes, it's King Lear. He's asking God why he has to play Trump the next hand."

"I don't blame him," Jason said. "What a come down. Probably better than Murdoch, though." He smiled irrelevantly at his host. "I guess that's it, huh?"

And Jason was gone. That's what Mimi had thought. When she realized that he was still alive, she was grateful. "Oh, you didn't die, thank god," she said. "What would I have told my friends?" She looked down in her lap. "But something died."

Down to Earth

"Why are you looking at me that way?" Mimi – her last name didn't matter – asked, her tone somewhere between curious and unnerved. "Is there something wrong? Do I have something in my hair?"

Jason Isaac's past-normal response would have been a pacifying, "Oh no, you look great" even if it weren't true. He decided that he would let her notice the ketchup on her forehead the next time she saw a mirror. But in this, his new life, literally sort of, he was more inside himself and looking out. This is important to the rest of the story and it would benefit you to get a some more definition of why.

Most everyone you ever meet, outside of an insane asylum – or those who should be inside – have two aspects to their being. The first is their real self and the second is the personality or ego. The self is the core person who has all the deeply personal thoughts, while the personality is the mask that the self puts up to interface with the world. The self might mention the ketchup; the personality would smile and say all is fine.

People produce these masks for themselves because the

species has been operated that way. We haven't reached a stage where everyone can drop their masks and deal with life directly. But that is our path. It won't do much for the cosmetics industry, but it will reduce war to a card game.

Jason intuitively understood this. Soon his cognitive mind would grasp it from a zillion different angles and it would be the centerpiece of his campaign to save the Earth, though he won't think of it in such grandiose terms, thank goodness. Meanwhile, back in reality, naked on his back, underneath but disconnected from Mimi in more than one way, he was looking not at the streak of ketchup but at her aura, which was now so blatantly apparent to him. Indeed, it was compelling for him to see it, stare at it, and his attention to her glow was what she was finding disquieting.

A point of context: Mimi was the widow of a chemist who had worked to develop methyl iodide, which was that extremely toxic pesticide that the large strawberry growers were insisting they needed to spray on their fields to produce decent-sized crops (read enormous profits). In hearings before the Bush EPA and the Schwarzenegger Department of Agri-cide (not their actual name) Mimi's husband and his cohorts insisted that the stuff was safe, that there was no need to worry about the (illegal alien) farm workers, or the (legal) children in the schools by the strawberry fields, forever.

Back at the lab, her poor deluded husband didn't notice that he had spilled a tiny drop of the stuff on his Big Mac and thus, two days later, Mimi was on the hunt again. She'd won an enormous out-of-court settlement from the Japanese firm that produced the stuff, so she wasn't looking for financial security but instead, you know, for fun. Jason had offered some promise in that department until a few pie-slice shaped seconds earlier, and now she found him looking at her strangely.

It didn't seem strange to Jason. He was in awe of his new vision. He was jarred partway back to reality by Mimi's distress, so he attempted to rejoin her but he just wasn't quite up to the task, emotionally. His head was an explosion of thoughts, with the dominant one being that he wanted to be alone as soon as possible so he might parse the massive synaptic display he thought of as his mind and get grounded. After all, he was back, here on Earth, where there was real ground. And he had work to do.

"Mimi, darling, um..." he started and then was briefly distracted again by her aura. He had watched is shift from a gently undulating wavy greenish color to a more erratic yellowish, but just then when he called her darling it calmed down considerably, for the moment. The long pause after the"um" wasn't helping, and no words were immediately coming to, um, mind. He grasped at a straw.

"I, uh, I don't know what's going on with me" -- that was more or less true – "but it might be those oysters." he nodded, as if he had convinced himself. Then he was distracted again as Mimi's aura started showing dancing orange flares, a lot like the ones the CHP puts in the road to warn of an accident. "I'm suddenly not feeling myself, a little dizzy."

"Oh poor baby," the wavy green returning as the maternal in Mimi bought the story. Hey, it was at least plausible. "Maybe I should go," she thought aloud. "I mean, and let you recover." She made a sound that was meant to be cute – a hungry snort sort of noise – and said, "We can pick this up later, okay?" With that she aimed a big wet kiss at Jason's mouth but at the last moment, an image of ecoli'd oysters sent her lips to his forehead. Then she climbed off Jason and the bed and headed for the bathroom. From whence there was an"Ooh, ugh!" followed by a rhetorical "Why didn't you tell me I had ketchup on my forehead!?!"

Jason was in his own world at that point and only managed

an unintelligible grunt. His mind was flipping back and forth from the all-consuming fact of his recent trip to wherever and the assignment he'd accepted to the challenge of getting Mimi out of his house as quickly as possible without being impolite. He was suddenly taken aback by how that was important to him. He rued his disingenuity toward the woman, realizing that such a fib, as reasonable as it might have seemed in his past life, did not feel comfortable to him in his new life. He took a deep breath and expelled it, trying to send the jumble of thoughts vying for his attention out with it.

The scope of his acclimatization from who he'd been to who he was suddenly seemed beyond comprehension, but then he was mollified by the notion that it should be. "I mean," he said to himself, "I was dead, and now I'm back, and I'm different. Lighten up, dickhead!" he ordered himself. He closed his eyes and focused his mind on breathing deeply into his *hara*. (The hara is the Japanese word for center, meaning the center of the body. Martial artists breathe into their hara to calm their mind.)

It actually worked quite well for him for a moment. Then Mimi was padding over to the bed, mewling, "Oh, my poor Jason. I'm so sorry you're not feeling well. But I know how you feel. I had food poisoning and I had the runs for a week. Icky-poo."

Jason peeked out at her and posted an appreciative if weakish smile on his face. "Thank you for being so understanding, Mimi," he offered.

"That's the way the world turns," she said thoughtfully, and then told him, "Well, gotta run." Then added, "Oops, wrong word. Sorry." She waved to him from the bedroom door and seconds later he heard the front door open and close.

"Oh, my," he said aloud, just to make sure, perhaps, that he was still there, still alive. Some more slow deep breaths, and then he decided, aloud, "It's time to get organized." He slid his legs out from under the covers and put his feet on the floor. "That's a good start," he told himself with a chuckle as he headed for the bathroom. He turned on the shower and got in without waiting for the hot water to arrive. He'd never done that before. "This is gonna get interesting," he told himself.

Usually Jason lingered in the shower. He enjoyed the tingling of the shower on his skin, and found the shower to be a place where new ideas came to him. He attributed the fact to negative ions, for which there was considerable scientific foundation but which isn't important to this story. And this morning he didn't want more thoughts. The shower was a transition for him. He washed and rinsed quickly, dried himself off and headed to the kitchen in his bathrobe.

But on his way he took a turn into his office where he turned on his computer. It seemed like forever that it booted up, but that was nothing new. When it finally was ready for him, he opened his browser and went to a news site. A pleased smile widened across his face as he saw that he could see auras around photographs. He snapped on his televison to a news channel and was further delighted to see auras on the live news readers as well as the people they reported about on tape.

He flicked around the news channels and chuckled. The Fox casters showed a marked difference in their auras from the broadcast networks, and even from CNN. Their auras were more of a orange-reddish hue and very static-y. The CNN auras were less of both, while the people on ABC were more of the green tinge and more stable. None of the auras was very solid nor very thick.

Jason went back to the computer and pulled up a clip of Jon Stewart being interviewed by Chris Wallace. "Oh, my," he said aloud for the second time that morning, as he observed the comedian to have a thick, solid blue-green aura while the faux newsman's oscillated dramatically through washed out yellows. "That's a clue, isn't it?" Gazing off toward the netherworld of answers, Jason caught a reflection of himself in the glass of a framed photograph. He turned on his heel and headed back to the bathroom. He was a sight to behold. His aura was akin to Stewart's blue-green and solid, but it seemed to fluctuate more. "He probably knows himself better than I do," Jason thought. "This morning he does." And then he added. "Not surprising, considering," and he headed down to the kitchen.

He got down the stairs and was headed for the kitchen, but instead he diverted to the living room where he pulled open a drawer in the trestle table in front of the couch from which he snagged a legal pad and a pen. Finally he made it to the center for culinary enterprise. As a writer, he had writing implements including pads of different sizes all over the house, but the pads in the kitchen were notably small, and he knew that small wouldn't do this morning. Indeed as he made himself an omelet and toast and coffee, and cut up a cantaloupe that truth was underlined as virtually every other action was writing something down on the pad. Similarly, when he sat down at the table-for-two in the breakfast nook, he alternated between bites and notes.

To set the literal stage briefly, Jason had been digging himself out from a deep financial hole for several years, and even when he had socked away a bunch of money it was clear to him that he was better off renting than buying a house. This was because where he wanted to live – in a better neighborhood on the Monterey Peninsula – was on the pricey side, and because he was confident that the economy was going to be sucking eggs for a while. And that was before he got the word from above. So he had found a wonderful cottage in the Skyline Forest area of Monterey, above the city, with an expansive view to the north and east that included both a large piece of The Bay and the airport.

He couldn't enjoy the view from the main floor of the house, which was a large single open room under a twelve foot ceiling that had separate area for sitting and talking, dining and cooking. Off from the kitchen area on one side was a tiny all-glass atrium with the breakfast table, and on the other side was a long wall behind which was a closet, a pantry/storage space, and a full bathroom. A staircase led to a single bedroom, a second bedroom which Jason used as his office, and the master bathroom. It was from those two rooms that the view opened up.

The situation was ideal for Jason because of the privacy. His cottage was on an over-sized lot, separate from the main house by a high hedge of holly bushes. The property was owned by a retired surgeon whose book was the second Jason had written under contract; a fascinating story of a selfless man who had served three tours in Vietnam patching up soldiers, many of whom wouldn't have gotten back to The States alive if it hadn't been for his skills and dedication.

Jason and the doctor lived well together, especially because the man spent ten months of the year with his daughter and son-in-law in Costa Rica, where he gave twenty hours a week of his time at a local clinic for Indians. This gave Jason even more privacy, and another benefit. The man had a dog, and it was Jason's responsibility to take care of Apollo – a yellow lab and something – while the doctor was out. It wasn't a responsibility but a great pleasure. Jason and The Dawg – he preferred that appellation better than his name – had bonded instantly with the animal spending most of his time, even when the doctor was home, at Jason's.

As if then on cue, The Dawg nuzzled against a special lever and let himself in the back door. "Oh...my...god," Jason said, his mouth open as he observed the beautiful blue aura around Apollo. The Dawg smiled at him.

Homework

By the time he had finished breakfast, and the dishes and pans were drying in the rack, Jason had also compiled such a lengthy to-do list that he was ready to rest his brain. He knew that wouldn't happen but he knew the best place to enjoy the mental gymnastics that would continue to plague him was on the beach. "Yo, Dawg, beach?" It was a rhetorical question. The only thing The Dawg didn't understand was why they didn't live on the beach and save the commute. Jason opened the door of his 2001 Miata and The Dawg climbed into the passenger seat. He was eighty pounds, so he filled the space. Jason got in and drove them up to Route 68 and then down to and through the Morse Gate into Pebble Beach, to the parking lot at the beach by Spanish Bay.

This was their regular spot. They walked a mile to the north end of Pebble Beach which bordered on the Asilomar Beach which was controlled by the state and where they enforced dog leash laws. At that point they turned around, passed by the parking lot, and headed another mile south, past China Rock, to a picnic table above the rocky shore where Jason sat for a while and The Dawg explored the gorse for rabbits and squirrels which he never chased.

The Dawg was a great chick magnet, of course. He was six but he still had a lot of puppy spirit in him. Not the jumping up kind – he was the epitome of well-behaved – but a hail-fellow-well-met spirit who presumed everyone was a good person. Except those who weren't whom he sniffed out at a distance and didn't approach, preferring to stand behind Jason in such cases.

They didn't run into many of that type on their walk since it was such a beautiful spot, and those who were visitors were gracefully overcome by the loveliness of the scenery and the gentle power of the ocean. Jason and The Dawg weren't themselves quite so overcome, but were still a little, every day, regardless of the weather. It was the nature of nature that got them all; well, most of them.

As you might imagine, the walk they took that day had an ancillary purpose. It was to check out the auras of the people on the beach. As expected, most of them were displaying a peaceful tone – they were, after all, walking by the Pacific – and Jason observed that was demonstrated not in the color but in the quality of the aura; its width and its solidity. The colors were mostly in the green family, which through further comparison was an indication of a higher order of awareness. Of course, that's why they had come to the beach.

There was only one person whom they encountered who moved The Dawg into his defensive position behind Jason. It was a man who clearly had a screw or two loose. There had been an occasion when Jason had placed himself between the man and another fellow who was a regular on the path when it appeared that angry words might degenerate into something physical. Jason's intervention had likely prevented fisticuffs, and in fact the screw-loose man had expressed gratitude to Jason for his courage to get between the two. But later he had for some reason changed his mind – or what there was of it – and would henceforth glare at Jason whenever they had seen each other.

Jason smiled at the man as they passed. He didn't do it to deliberately irk the fellow. He just didn't feel that glaring accomplished anything. This time he kept his face blank as he observed the man's aura. It was orange with squiggly black lines shooting through it. It reminded him of a power line downed by a tree in a storm, sparking and bouncing in the street. After they had passed the man and The Dawg had moved back to his lead position, Jason said, "So that's what crazy looks like," and The Dawg emitted something of a af-firming growl.

Back in the car after their constitutional, man and dog re-turned home. The Dawg had some serious napping to do, and Jason sat down at his computer to fill out some of his direct experience of seeing the auras of some more people in today's headlines with some of those from the past. Some of the obvious moments were Ted Kennedy after Chappaquid-dick, Nixon saying "I am not a crook," and Clinton during the intern sex scandal. He also checked on some confessed criminals, and others who professed their innocence. Pat-terns were clear and most of his presumptions were con-firmed.

Then Jason went about screening images of actors, people of different professions, different ages, genders, cultures, and educational levels. He had spent most of two days – minus meals and perambulating, but not taking phone calls – researching every variable he thought important, when he thought to give a call to the fellow who was producing the video on PSR, thinking he might illuminate any major holes Jason had missed in his novelty and compulsion.

As it turned out, the guy, also a journalist, wasn't difficult to reach. Most journalists aren't. They don't have to hide because no one is looking for the work they do anymore. That's how Tony Seton explained it when Jason found his website and called the number at the bottom of the page.

Jason's intuition had served him well, he had covered most of the appropriate ground. Still, Tony offered up a couple of useful points. "First, you have to understand that we all have the ability, innately, to see auras. It's just that we are talked out of them by our parents. 'No, honey there is no red paint around that man.' So generation after generation we grow up with this enormously valuable tool denied to us. That might be why we're so schizophrenic today. Probably why people are hiding in insane asylums; there's too much conflict in their minds with the outside world.

"But the good news," the fellow journalist continued, "is that as we approach an evolutionary shift – that's The Professor's opinion, and I agree with him – many people are becoming intuitively aware that they are seeing people differently.

"Second, no one can fake their aura. No one. We looked at every major public figure from Dick Cheney to Lindsay Lohan, O. J. Simpson to the top dogs at Goldman, Sachs. You could see clearly in their character charting that they never exceeded a certain color level, even when they were telling the truth. Kissinger was my favorite. Until The Professor fiddled with his numbers, virtually every time he opened his mouth his character level said he was lying. Even when we knew he was telling the truth. The man cared so little for the truth, it didn't matter to him if he was speaking it.

"But I think The Professor got the algorithms fine-tuned now to a point where he could tell better than the person himself whether or not he was telling the truth."

"I get the sense that people can think they're being honest, at least in the surface of their mind, but if deep down they know the truth, or doubt what they're saying, it will show up as scattering in the foundation of the aura."

"That's right," Tony said. "And if they don't know but think they do, deep down, it shows at the top edge of the aura. There has to be congruity between their thinking and their feeling selves, or lights go off, figuratively speaking."

"When is your video going to be released?" Jason asked him.

"Dunno. Not to sound cagey, but there are some issues that I can't get into with you right now, not on the phone. But some time this fall I expect."

"You haven't asked why I'm interested," Jason said, and he heard a chuckle at the other end of the line.

"I have worked with The Professor for over six months now, and I think I can do almost as well as his computer at sussing out most people. I can tell that you are an honest person and your questions sure indicate a high level of consciousness. Maybe some day you'll be back up in Marin or I'll come down there and you can tell me over lunch. Or not. Your call."

"That's most gracious of you. Thank you," Jason said. "I look forward to our getting together. And I will be able to tell you what is my interest in all this."

"That's fine. I know we're on the same side."

When Jason hung up the phone, he was very pleased with how far he'd gotten with what he saw as the first stage of his project, whatever that was. He was understanding how to read auras from a cognitive perspective, and he imagined that it wouldn't be too long before he would know someone without thinking about their aura. His intuition would read people without his having to consider the factors of their aura.

"I think we've come far, my friend," Jason said to The Dawg, who was lying down in the maroon dog bed on the floor in a back corner of the office. Jason had four different dog beds around the cottage each a different color, which was kinda funny since dogs are color blind. Anyway, The Dawg opened one eye, looked at Jason and made a sound, probably through his nose, that represented an acknowledgment of being consulted. It was enough for Jason.

In more ways than one. "I think we should take a break from the homework, old chum. I thought maybe of picking something up downtown, but I'd rather stay home and watch one of the *Thin Man* movies. You haven't seen Asta in a while. We'll watch the one with Jimmy Stewart and that slut dog Mrs. Asta with the black puppy." Another nose sound, maybe a snort above acknowledgment toward pleasure. It was tough not to please this dog in Jason's house.

The Guide

It was late the next morning, and before Jason and The Dawg went for their beach walk, that Jason asked him to indulge him for ten minutes while he popped in at the Aquarium to check on the auras in the big fish tank. This being Saturday and August, the tourists had descended and parking was nigh on impossible, so Jason left his car in a tiny parking lot by a friend's office, two blocks from the Aquarium. The friend had two young children and it was unlikely that he would be in the office on a Saturday. Anyway, he would know Jason's car if he came upon it, and that Jason wouldn't be long having left The Dawg in the car. It wasn't a heat issue since Monterey in August was under the marine layer at least until noon and usually through the day.

The day before, Jason had been checking out the aura of everyone he set eyes on. That had abated as his mind was on the next step, and he didn't know what that next step was. He felt like Harrison Ford when he had to cross the abyss to save Sean Connery's life. He just put his foot out and it came down on something. Jason didn't feel danger; on the contrary, he felt good and confident. And comfortable not knowing where his foot would fall next.

Jason showed his press pass and was welcomed through the main gate. He strolled over to the big tank and copped a corner of a bench off to one side and looked at the fish and birds. It was as he suspected. Nothing from the fish, even the four-foot lemon shark, and just light reading from the birds.

After all, he wasn't Noah, he said to himself silently. It wasn't his job to bring along all of the animals. The more advanced mammals and some other creatures were able to sense the same qualities that appeared to people in auras. And once the population got back down to a healthy two billion or so, the animals along with the rest of nature would regain a healthy balance. His mind eschewing with a flash of humor, the Ark and its captain, Jason was suddenly aware that he was staring, not at the tank or its denizens but at a woman standing before it.

She was bending her maybe five-six frame slightly over a maybe ten-year-old boy, and pointing to what was inside the tank. She seemed to be explaining to the child what he was seeing. What Jason was seeing was a very attractive late-forties woman in jeans and a rugby shirt – probably from Land's End if he recognized the colors – and running shoes. She also wore a black wool pea jacket, which was smart because it was always cooler than anyone expected inside the Aquarium. The jacket was open to reveal a healthy figure, and atop it all was a large head of long raven curls, framing an oval face that Modigliani might have sketched.

When he was parsing the scene later, he wasn't sure which caught his eye first, the woman or her aura, but Jason was taken, too, by her marvelously strong cobalt blue aura that seemed unrufflable. That is, until she turned toward Jason, standing straight up, and giving him a long hard look. Then the blue lost some of its luster and the aura narrowed. This all happened with them 20 feet apart. When he realized that he had been staring and it had upset her, Jason held his palms up toward her and mouthed "I'm sorry." There was nothing else he could do but get up and leave, which is what he did. He returned to the car and told The Dawg what had happened. The Dawg gave him an unsympathetic snort as if to say, "I'm sniffing all the time; it never goes anywhere."

"Yes," Jason replied, "But you don't get nasty looks back." He pulled away from the Cannery Row tourist maelstrom and headed west. "To the beach," he announced but no one in the car took notice. It was a given where they were going.

The fog was low on the coast. They could barely make out Point Joe from the parking area only several hundred yards away. But there was no wind, so the air wasn't cold; more nestly, though not as warm as where he had been three days earlier. Jason made a deliberate effort not to think about what he was supposed to be thinking about since he didn't know. In the old days, maybe even four days earlier, that might have annoyed him, but not so much any more, if at all. He hadn't been greatly tested. The business with the woman at the Aquarium might have nagged at him before but it didn't today. Life goes on, as it were.

The boys returned to the car. "You don't mind if I make another stop, do you?" No answer from The Dawg. "I need a couple of things at Trader Joe's, and I'll buy something for dinner with a bone in it." An affirmative snort gave him permission. "Thank you, Dawg."

Five minutes later he was extracting himself from the Miata and bringing his used grocery bags in with him. He bought lamb chops for himself to share with The Dawg, garlic fries because he didn't expect to be seeing anyone in the next couple of days, some fresh fruit and vegetables, and a bottle of $6.99 Proseco champagne. It wasn't Veuve Cliquot but it wasn't bad, especially when he squeezed a blackberry from the vines along the back fence in his yard into the chilled glass before pouring.

Jason had made his way through the line, and was bagging his own groceries, when he noticed that the person behind him was the woman from the Aquarium. His jaw dropped. Her face, which was even prettier close up, turned to a scowl as it suddenly was when she recognized him. She was about to say something when the checker spoke up, "Hey, Mr. Isaac, that was a great book you did on Mrs. Ivers. You really caught her spirit. She's a good lady, good for the community. I really like what you did for her."

Jason was happily diverted. "Why thank you, Alyce. How nice of you to say. It was an honor to get to write her story. She deserved all the praise she's gotten."

The checker said, "I got your book for my mother for Christmas, too."

"Oh, neat," Jason said. "I'd be glad to autograph it for her if you want."

"Oh, Mr. Isaac, she'd love that," the young woman said enthusiastically. "Do you know when you're gonna be in here next?" she asked.

"When are you working next?"

"The next four days. Today is my Monday."

"How 'bout I stop by on the real Monday? But maybe they'll let you leave the book at the desk," he said, nodding in the direction of the management booth. "and then if we miss each other, I can sign it the next time I come in."

"Sure, they'll let me do that. Great. Thanks a lot."

"My pleasure," Jason said. "Leave a note in the book with her name."

"Wonderful," said a very pleased Alyce. "I'll do it!"

Jason picked up his bag, gave a nonintrusive smile to the

woman who had by this time, as the result of the conversation no doubt, lost her scowl, and he made his way out to the parking lot. He put the bag in the trunk, and on the way back home, he told The Dawg what happened.

When they pulled into the driveway and approached the cottage, Jason could hear the phone ringing. In the old days, he might have made an effort to race across the porch, throw open the door and catch the call before it went into voicemail. Not this day. He unloaded the grocery bag and put things away, folding the bag and leaving it by the front door to put back in the car. Then he went over to the phone and picked up the message. It was from his friend Cindy, the woman who had gotten him launched in biographies five years earlier. They had been friends and colleagues since, with Cindy managing the formatting of the books, and designing most of the covers.

The message said,"Dahling, where are you? I sent you an email a couple of days ago inviting you to a dinner party tonight. I need you, I need you. The husband of a friend of mine got stuck in Cincinnati for an extra week, so I'm down a guy. Can you help out, please, please, please? Six o'clock, coat-'n-tie, sit down dinner steaks on the grill. I'll send you home with a bunch of bones for The Dawg."

"Hah, she thinks that will swing it for me," Jason said as he hung up the phone. The Dawg gave a yawn. "Yeah, well you and she think alike." He picked up the phone again, punch a few buttons and had Cindy on the line in a trice.

"Oh, goody, I knew you wouldn't let me down. You know how I hate an imbalanced table, especially too many women. They talk, talk, talk."

"Bones for The Dawg is what did it. He said all right."

"Bless the pooch," she said. "See you at six." And she rang off. One of the reasons that they worked so well together was that she didn't waste time. Jason was pleased with the invitation. He hadn't had any real social contact since he'd said goodbye to Mimi. "That was another lifetime," he said to The Dawg who said nothing. He rarely acknowledged the obvious.

Part of Cindy's thing about not wasting time was that when she said six she meant six. There was no concept in her mind for fashionably late. Jason knocked on door of her Pacific Grove Craftsman house at exactly six. The door opened, and instead of it being Cindy it was – can you guess? – the woman from the Aquarium and TJ's. She was as startled to see him as he was to see her, but he was secretly more pleased.

"Uh, hi," she said and shook her head. "I don't believe this. It's you." She stood aside and let him come in. He tried not to be obvious but he walked slowly enough so his journalist's eagle eye could take her all in. Actually, it wasn't the journalist but the man who noted her lovely simple black dress, a large cranberry leather belt with a large silver buckle, matching cranberry low-heeled shoes, and a single strand of pearls hanging down toward a modestly-cut neckline.

"Hi honey, glad you could make it," came a cry from Cindy in the kitchen. Jason waved at her and then turned back to the woman who had let him in. "I'm terribly sorry about this morning at the Aquarium, I hadn't meant to stare." He offered his hand,"My name is Jason Isaac. I work with Cindy on book projects."

The woman took his hand. "Carole Holley," she told him, her eyes never leaving his. And that was all they said for perhaps thirty seconds, as they stood looking and holding each other's hand.

"How do you do?" Jason said, and then shook her hand.

"Fine thank you," she said and looked down at her hand. She loosened her grip, he loosened his, and their hands came apart. "It was all right, this morning I mean. You didn't do anything wrong." She laughed. "I just moved up her from Los Angeles a week ago and I'm not used to living in a civilized place yet."

He laughed. "Welcome to the Monterey Peninsula."

"Thank you," she said.

"Where are you living?" he asked. Then he quickly added,"It's all right to ask that here."

She laughed again. "I'm house-sitting for a friend of mine, Joan, who lives up on the ridge near the mouth of Carmel Valley. She was on a three-month shoot in Japan of a documentary and they're phasing out nuclear power, maybe, and now she's back in LA editing."

"And then you're going back to LA," Jason asked, letting a hint of disappointment sound in his voice.

She heard it, and wasn't displeased. "No, I'm done with Southern California. I thought I'd try to find a place up here. I've visited a lot and every time I've left I've wondered why. Now I'm not going to wonder."

"Oh that's neat."

"Thank you," she said.

A thought caught Jason. "Excuse me, I hope this doesn't come out the wrong way, but when Cindy called me, she said I was filling in because a husband was stuck in Cincinnati." He left it there.

Carole took just a moment to get his question. "Oh, oh no, my goodness." She laughed again. "I would never be married to a man who might get stuck in Cincinnati."

The relief on Jason's face was palpable as they both laughed. "And so that wasn't your son at the Aquarium?"

"No children either. That was just a boy who attached himself to me, thinking I might know something, about what was in the tank."

Jason smiled at her. "I can understand the boy's inclination. Not about the fish tank specifically."

Carole blushed. "Are you usually this direct?" It wasn't a complaint but a legitimate question.

Jason was direct. "A few days ago I was told that I would meet someone very important for what I was doing. There was no other clue. When I asked who that person was or how I would know him or her, the answer was, I would know." He let that sink in for a moment and then continued. "When I saw you this morning. I, I just felt a connection. It was different. It wasn't lust, it was a knowingness. At least that's what I thought, and then when you saw me looking at you and it obviously was displeasing and I left, I had no thought that I was ever to see you again."

"And that lasted what, two hours?"

"Yeah, something like that. When I saw you at Trader Joe's I wanted to explain, but I couldn't get the words out. Usually I'm glib, but when I saw you again, I couldn't speak."

"I didn't give you a chance. That was my fault. I'm sorry."

"Oh no, please," Jason told her. "And you opened the door here tonight and lights went on and bells went off, and there was no room left to think."

Carole laughed. "Good line. So what are you doing that you were expecting to meet someone?"

Before Jason could answer, Cindy joined them, smiling. "I thought you two might hit it off."

Dinner was a marvelous affair, and the beginning of one, but let's not get ahead of ourselves. As Jason learned during the course of the evening, Carole had been a freelance copywriter, working with the top advertising firms on the West Coast. She had been married briefly before she left New York – Queens, to be precise – twenty years earlier. This information came from Cindy during one of the few times he and Carole weren't together. Cindy had met her through mutual friends in graphic design around the time Carole had arrived on the West Coast, and had been working on her since to move up to Monterey. Confirming Jason's first impression, she said she thought her friend was 45-ish.

During the hour that lead up to dinner, Carole worked the door, welcoming the other six guests – there were to be nine altogether, with Cindy at the head of the table – who all arrived within fifteen minutes of the appointed hour. Jason made sure everyone had a libation. They got together for short conversations, and otherwise made an effort to circulate. After each assault in the purpose of politesse, they circled around and managed to run into each other again.

Then it was time for dinner, and Carole and Jason were seated across from each other. Again they did their best to converse with others at the table, but it wasn't easy since they were only interested in each other. Perhaps you can remember when you were struck by the magic. Remember the scene from *West Side Story*, the dance at the gym when Maria and Tony see each other across the room. The lights have gone down and there is a spotlight on each of them. They are alone and come together.

When the evening came to an end, Jason walked Carole to her car. She opened her door and the two stood together, not very far apart. "You never told me what it was you were going to be doing, that you needed to find someone for."

Jason looked down in silence. Carole said, "I'm sorry, I

didn't mean to push you or anything. You don't have to tell me, surely."

Jason looked up into her face. "There was a scene in *The Razor's Edge* where Bill Murray, in a very powerful, serious role, speaks of a woman who had come into his life but who had died. And he said of her, 'I thought she was my reward.'"

Carole was startled. "What are you saying? That there is danger. That you're worried about my safety? I couldn't believe that."

Jason shook his head, "No, nothing like that. It's more than a reward. It's good, it's alive, it's important, it's huge. I just, I just never realized that there could be you. You're an extraordinary woman, and an incredible human being. I somehow knew that when I saw you the first time this morning but I couldn't get my mind around it."

Carole showed some resistance. "This isn't I-love-you-but-we-can't-be-together, is it?"

Jason shook his head, slowly and fondly. "No, it's just incredible, and I want to tell you everything, but I couldn't do it tonight, at a dinner party. "You need to trust me until I can explain. I promise you it will be worth it."

He felt her eyes pore over his face, he opened his eyes to his soul so that she could be assured.

Her face slowly melted into a smile, and her eyes glistened. "Oh my," she said, and then had to clear her throat. "No one has ever done that for me before." She teetered forward, he put his arms around her so that she wouldn't fall. She wouldn't. Then their faces closed the distance between them, their lips meeting softly, purposefully, exploring, confirming.

Reluctantly Carole pulled away, taking Jason's hands in

hers. "This will have to wait," she said and immediately added,"until tomorrow, if you are free."

Jason nodded. Carole got into her car. Jason closed her door. She started the engine and opened the window. "Just so you know," she began, and put the car in gear but had her foot on the brake.

"Yes?"

"Yes," she echoed. "You found who you were looking for."

The Morning After

Jason's phone rang at 7:30 the next morning. He'd already been up for an hour, since the sun mostly dictated his arisal time. It was Carole. She sounded still half asleep but still managed a full-tilt Brooklyn accent. "So, like, uh, weren't you gonna ask me out, or what?"

"Victorian Corner in PG for brunch?"

"Okay," she said, brightly, the sleep and accent instantly gone. "I think I was there once, on Lighthouse, right? Nice place."

"That's right. When would be good for you?"

Back to the accent, "I don't know. You're the one asking me out, huh?"

"And a walk on the beach with The Dawg afterwards?"

"Of course, of course."

"And you'll wear your Sunday sneakers."

"What else?"

"That should do it." They laughed. "A half-hour too soon?"

"I don't think so. I was up most of the night."

"Oh. I'm sorry you didn't sleep well."

"Silly boy, I was smiling so much I couldn't sleep. Now will you get off the phone so I can be on time."

It being eight, and Jason closer, he arrived first and took a table in the front window. Carole was a minute or two early. He watched her pull her dark blue Prius into a slot across the street and walk toward the restaurant. She saw him in the window and waved to him. He waved back and stood as she came in the door. She was in jeans and a shirt with her pea coat again. "It was sunny on the ridge, and of course foggy down here," she reported as he helped her off with the coat and slipped it over the back of her chair. Then he pulled out her chair for and pushed it in when she had sat down.

"All night long," she said, as he regained his seat across from her, "I thought of you and how I felt. I played back all of our little conversations. I remembered your table manners, and, and..." she faltered, "and I remembered our first kiss. I almost wasn't going to wash my face. Do I sound like a kid, or what?" Then she peered across the table at him. "I'm not nuts, am I? I haven't gone overboard and you're just being polite?"

Jason broke into laughter, and before he could answer, the stately blonde owner of the restaurant came to the table. "Oh, Jason," she said, "how nice to see you. It's been too long."

"Good morning, Tricia," Jason said to her. "It's because I always clean my plate and The Dawg resents it."

"Oh, don't worry. I'll make a doggy bag for him. You can't eat it."

"Deal," Jason replied. "Tricia, I want you to meet Carole. Carole, this is Tricia." The women shook hands.

Tricia said, "This Jason, he is a very good man. I tell my Paul, who I married 38 years ago, he better stay on his toes, or

Jason and me..." and she left it there with a big smile for both of them. She put menus on the table, offered them water and coffee, and promised, "I'll be back."

"No," Jason said to Carole after the woman had left.

"No?" Carole asked.

"If you've gone overboard, then we're both in deep water."

"Ooh, I like. Tell me more. Did you sleep?"

"Like a log. I hope that's all right."

"Sleep is good, sleep is good. Did you dream?" Carole asked as Tricia arrived with the coffee.

"Of course he dreamed'" Tricia chimed in. "He dreamed of you."

Jason chuckled, "Tricia, please, we're not engaged yet. We only met last night."

Carole corrected him, "It was more like yesterday, and it was three times."

Tricia raised her eyebrows. "Oh, sounds like fate to me. Wave me down when you are ready to order," she said, and left.

Carole picked up her menu and read the choices. "I think I had Belgian waffles with fresh berries last time. Very good. I'll have those again."

Jason waved to Tricia. She acknowledged him and came over when she finished with another table. "So let me guess. Carole wants the Belgian waffles with the blueberries and strawberries?" Then, "What?" she asked the surprised faces.

"Do you have a microphone under the table?" Carole asked. "How did you know? That's amazing."

Tricia smiled. "Yeah, it's going around. Something in the

40

air." She turned to Jason who ordered the eggs Benedict. "Champagne with that?"

Carole shook her head, and Jason said, "Another time, Tricia." The woman left.

"How did she do that?" Carole asked him. "You didn't signal her. I was watching you."

"No more amazing than our meeting yesterday."

"Three times," Carole reminded him. "While I was awake last night because of you, I wondered what it was that you were talking about. What you were doing, and why you thought I might help."

"Did you come up with anything?"

"Tons of stuff, but none of it stuck."

"How about saving the world?" Jason asked lightly.

Carole nodded,"That would be a two-person job, I think."

Jason grimaced, "It's going to sound strange, Carole."

She reached her hands across the table and took his hands, and waiting until he'd brought his smile to bear from his hands holding hers to her eyes, she said, "I've already said yes, Jason."

"How did you know?"

"I don't know the details, but I know our connection. It's unlike anything I've known before, in my head or my heart. This is one of those meant-to-be things. Whatever it is, it fits both of us." She let go of his hands and leaned back in her chair. "How could it be otherwise?"

Jason looked out the window for a long moment and then back at Carole. "I was afraid that maybe you'd wake up this morning and get a new phone number or something.

Because it felt so powerful."

"Like the Greek gods couldn't touch a mortal or they would burn up?"

"Yes."

"Maybe we're not mortal? You know, sort of."

Jason took a deep breath. "Funny you should say that."

And then for the next two hours, Jason told Carole what had happened to him, and then about his research with auras. At each point of possible incredulity, she merely nodded her head in accord. When he had finished, the breakfast dishes had been long cleared away and they had switched from coffee to tea, Jason felt enormously relieved. "It sounded crazy before I told you, but having met you, and telling you everything, it doesn't sound so crazy."

Again Carole reached across the table for Jason's hands. "I remember a story about the philosopher Abraham Maslow speaking to a class of British high school age students." He said, 'Who among you is going to be great?' and no one raised their hand. Then he said, 'Who else then?'"

"Yes indeed," Jason said. "Who else then?"

"Jason, what's it like up there?" Carole asked.

"A lot like Carmel in terms of weather. A lot of fog, but most of it is already on the ground, and it's not as chilly somehow. Warm dry fog," he told her.

"Sounds like something a caterer would offer at an Eskimo wedding." They both laughed

Jason added, "A lot of dogs up there, mostly lying around, gnawing on large bones, watching movies. *Best in Show* is one of the clear favorites, but they also like Asta in the six *Thin Man* films, and the Benji films, of course."

He took another deep breath. "So...ready for a walk?"

Carole nodded her head. "Yes, and to meet The Dawg."

Jason caught Tricia's eye and nodded. She went back into the kitchen and came back with a take-out container and the check. "The bones," she said, putting them on the table. "I promised for The Dawg."

"I'll tell him who they are from, Tricia. Thank you."

"Always a pleasure to have you in the front window. You bring in all the nice people." She paused and clasped her hands together as she looked at Carole. "And today you brought this fine lady with you. Good boy. My Paul, he won't worry any more."

They all laughed. Jason put cash on the table, and then stood and helped Carole with her coat. "I think you'll need this on the beach, my dear."

As Carole got her hands through the sleeves, she took Jason's hands and pulled his arms around her and leaned her head against his shoulder. "Jason?" she asked quietly.

"Yes, Carole?"

"You know when I met you this morning?"

"Yes, Carole."

"And you didn't kiss me?"

"Yes, Carole."

"I liked that. I like that you didn't presume to kiss me this morning."

"Carole?"

"Yes, Jason?"

"It wasn't easy, except that as of a couple of days ago, along

43

with everything else, I'm not taking anything for granted. I don't want to. It's far more grand to experience it fresh and in the moment. That way it never gets old, if that makes sense."

"Jason?"

"Yes, Carole."

"That makes sense." She turned in his arms, looked into his face, and then kissed him quickly on the lips. "You left a twenty-dollar tip. Always leave them wanting more," she said, taking his arm and leading him out onto the street, "except me, of course." They walked to her car. She got into the driver's seat, leaving the door open this time.

"I'll get my car, and pull around in front of you and you can follow me," Jason offered.

"Anywhere," she told him in a throaty voice. Jason hesitated, then closed her door and went to get his car.

It was love at first sight, Carole and The Dawg. How could it have been otherwise; they each being such marvelous creatures. "Doesn't The Dawg need a leash?" Carole asked as they were leaving the parking lot for the beach.

"Nah," said Jason. "I heel when he barks."

Carole put her hand in Jason's and they started off. "I can't remember ever feeling so, so in synch with my life. Do you know what I mean?"

"I had that feeling myself for the first time last night. When you opened the door for me, when we kissed. And this morning, every minute of our being together, how you understood what I said, and without any confusion or skepticism. Yes, synch, you and I."

"But I have to ask you," Carole said.

"Yes, my dear?"

"I heard everyone calling her Sandy and you, we, called her Tricia."

Jason chuckled. "I asked her about her name being Sandy. It wasn't typical from someone from Italy. She told me that her real name was Silviatricia, but when she was first here as a teenager and didn't know much English and a friend was helping her to find a job, the friend told her to pick a simple name because Silviatricia was too hard to pronounce. The friend suggested Sandy and it stuck. She never changed it, but she told me that she likes Tricia better."

"So Tricia it is. I like that story," she added rubbed her body against his while she walked.

"Carole?"

"Yes, Jason."

"This may seem like an odd question, considering the feelings that have been flying about since we met..."

"And here we are walking on the beach holding hands?"

"Just so."

"And?"

"I, I guess I'm surprised that you aren't, uh, taken? If that doesn't sound presumptuous, it's just that this feels so good, and I'm not looking for holes in it or anything."

"Well how about you, you wonderful woman? It doesn't seem like anyone has your heart."

He looked at her while they were still walking and shook his head, and they walked on in silence for a while before Carole spoke; quietly, in a reflective voice.

"There was someone. A good guy. We had fun together."

"But?"

"But it wasn't compelling. Does that sound harsh?" She looked up at him.

"No, no it doesn't. There are different levels of relationships. I've been sociable but not involved for years. Never like this. Nothing close."

"Uh-huh. Well just so you know, my relationship with him ended last night. When I opened the door and saw you standing there, as surprised, and as delighted as I was. After the thing at Trader Joe's, I looked you up on line and confirmed that you weren't a stalker, and that you were as special as I felt.

"The relationship with Maury was headed south, if you'll pardon the pun. I had told him that I was probably going to stay in Monterey. He's a lighting guy, very good at what he does and he loves what he does. He wouldn't move, and I thought my relocating would officially put the kibosh on it, but we hadn't said that to each other."

Jason waited, hearing in her voice that there was more.

"So one of the things I did last night when I couldn't sleep was I sent him an email. He won't be surprised. And it wasn't monogamous, I don't think, not for him anyway." She let that sink in and then asked,"Does that tell you what you wanted to know, Mr. Isaac?" she asked with a tease in her voice.

"I feel like I'm racing to catch up with myself. The words, the feelings are beyond everything I've known, everything I've read or heard about. I want to be perfect with you. That sounds sorta lame, but I don't know how else to say it. I've never felt so called to perform – to be my best self – ever."

They had stopped walking and were facing each other. Carole took both his hands in hers, and asked him, "So like given the choice between saving the world and exploring a relationship with me...loving and being loved in a way we never imagined was possible...then it's 'Sorry world?'"

Jason nodded. "Pretty much, yeah. I mean, it might be possible to do both. Can this saving the world thing be a full-time job?"

"I can't imagine," Carole agreed, shaking her head.

"No, plus, for this to be like a long-term thing, I think we'll need to have some place to do it. And as nice as heaven is, at least the part I saw, it doesn't hold a candle to this beach."

Carole nodded her head sagely. "Good point. Maybe we should we ask The Dawg?"

"Good idea." Jason saw him roaming by the water's edge. "Yo," he called. The Dawg's ears went up, he turned his head to determine where it was coming from and then trotted back to them. He stood before them, his mouth open, tongue hanging out, wagging his tail, waiting patiently.

"Yo, Dawg, Carole and I think we're perfect together."

"And we want your blessing," Carole added.

The Dawg barked three times. "Oh, of course," Jason said, bending down and rubbing his head. "The three of us."

"Woof," Carole said.

Where Do We Start

The Dawg was happy to have Carole in the mix. He attributed to her the fact that the walkie that morning was longer, and Jason was paying less attention to where he went and what he pretended to chase. The Dawg considered the birds on the beach to be his trainers, or at least his exercise partners. He ran toward them and after them but never with the intent of catching them. They didn't know that so they gave him a good run.

Meanwhile, Carole and Jason walked together, thoroughly engrossed in conversation, and each other. Sometimes they held hands, sometimes they just bumped into each other. Someone watching them wouldn't have known if they were old friends or new lovers, or both.

Much of their talking was about themselves, as might be expected, with Jason offering his insight as a journalist on the world and where it was stuck, and eliciting from Carole her communications experience.

"I don't know why they thought I would be useful in this enterprise," she said. "You know what's going on and what needs to be done. I write advertising jingles. I sell things."

She paused and then said, "Oh, so maybe my role is to sell you, or your ideas. Hah! that would be neat. All this time I didn't know what I was doing, and I was getting ready for the biggest sales job in the history of the world. That works," she said.

"That's good because that's the last thing I know how to do. Especially selling myself."

"Why do you suppose that is, Jason? You've accomplished so much."

Jason shrugged, "I don't know. It's not humility. I've done a lot, been around a lot of history being made. I guess it always seemed that my role was as an observer. I wasn't part of the history. Does that make sense?"

"To you perhaps," she said and bumped into him for punctuation.

"I'm glad you didn't have champagne at breakfast, you'd be falling all over the place."

"Nope, just against you."

"Oh, that's okay then."

"Jason, do you have any sense of how much time we have?"

He shook his head. "No idea, but I think there's enough. I don't think this would have happened – me being pulled up there, our connecting – unless it was all supposed to work out. Of course that may sound selves-serving – you like that? serving our two selves – but I've felt for a long time, like you, what you said, that I was going down this path for a purpose, even if I didn't know what it was."

Carole was looking down at the sand as they walked. Jason felt that she was pulling thoughts together and didn't speak. She took his hand. "The more we talk about where we've been and who we are, the more obvious it becomes how perfectly we fit together."

"Do you think this is what they had in mind," he asked with a nod toward the heavens, "when they said I'd have someone to work with?"

"So far," Carole replied in a soft voice.

After two hours, they found themselves back at the parking lot and their two cars. Jason asked Carole, "So, you want to maybe come up to my place, and we can talk some more? If you're not busy?"

"You died and came back to life on a mission to save the world, we fall totally in love, and you ask me if I'm busy?"

"Perhaps booked would have been a better word? And maybe rise instead of fall."

"'Rise in love.' Uh-huh. Probably need to check that one out. Do you want to show me where you live, Jason?" she ask coyly.

"Maybe. I was up all night cleaning, just in case, you know."

"I thought you said you were sleeping?"

"I multi-task. I dust and polish and The Dawg pushes around the vacuum cleaner."

"I see. Hmm. Well, maybe I should pop by then and give the place a white glove inspection. I should know who I'm dealing with, after all."

"After what all? We just got started."

"I'm not sure that you can take that literalist stuff on the road, okay?"

"Do you have your white gloves with you?" Jason asked with as much innocence as he could muster.

"Of course."

"Of course? What are you, a Jewish American Princess?"

"If you must know, I not Jewish. I'm not any religion. I am an American. I was born in East Providence which has one of the largest Portugese communities in the United States."

"I read that they sell more Mateus wine per capita in Rhode Island than any other state."

"My parents were both born in this country and both sets of grandparents came from the Canary Islands."

"That explains your absolutely stunning skin color."

"Thank you. And as regards the royalty issue, I asked my parents to stop calling me princess five years ago, when I was 40. They're pretty good about it, at least when I'm with them, but it's been tough for them."

"So you'll follow me?"

"Do you need to ask?"

Jason opened her car door and Carole got into the driver's seat. Before she closed the door she said to him, huskily, "I hope it's not too far."

Jason got The Dawg and himself into his car, and soon the two-car convoy was weaving through the back roads of Pebble Beach, and out the Morse Gate. Five minutes later they arrived at his house. Jason pulled into his driveway and Carole parked behind him. He watched her take in the estate, as he called it, with the main house, the large yard, and his cottage. The delight was evident in her face.

"Jason, this is lovely," she said as she joined him at his car where he was letting The Dawg out. "It has a wonderful feeling. It's good. It feels very secure, if you know what I mean."

"I'm glad you like it, too." He guided her up the short

flagstone pathway to the short porch and front door where The Dawg was waiting for them.

"I think he's excited to have me here, Jason."

"Oh yes, he loves to show off his vacuuming."

Jason moved ahead and opened the door, but only a crack. "Yo, Dawg, where are your manners. Lady's first."

The Dawg moved back a couple steps and Jason opened the door for Carole, who crossed the threshold with a big smile, shaking her head. She walked into the living room several paces and looked around. "Oh my," she said as her eyes scanned the room. "What a great place, Jason. And Dawg," she added looking at the animal entering the house with Jason following and closing the door behind them.

"You like it?"

"I'd say it's darling but that would sound too feminine, especially with two males living here, but it is so very comfortable. No Leroy Neiman's cluttering the walls pretending to be art."

"Hardly," Jason chuckled.

Carole was walking around the room looking at Jason's eclectic hangings. "Modigliani, Vespigniani, oh, and I think that's a Bernard Ganter, isn't it?"

"That's right. I once had a gig selling art at a gallery in Carmel and took part of my payment in a couple of pieces that weren't moving."

"I saw an exhibition of his work in Paris years ago. He never became hugely popular, or expensive, but I liked his style."

"And this," she said stopping in front of a pair of prints. "Very nice, but I don't recognize them."

"I got those in Mendocino years ago. A Japanese artist; I

don't remember his name. That never matters to me. It's what I like to see on my walls."

"Very nice."

"When I was looking at them in a gallery up there, the gallery director, I think she was, came up to me and said in hushed tones that the artist was very ill. You know, that he was likely to die and drive the prices through the roof."

Carole chuckled. "Oh my."

"So I asked her, 'You mean he's not dead though?' and she admitted, with some sincere regret it seemed, that he was still among the breathing. So I got both prints for a song."

Carole was standing in the kitchen area looking back toward the front of the house. Jason saw her eyes go to the staircase and then back to him. They looked at each other for what must have been a minute though it might have seemed much longer, or like no time at all.

"Would you like to get physical?" Jason asked her.

Carole laughed.

"That's funny?"

Carole shook her head. "So you can read my mind, too? Not just see my aura?"

"Why do you say that?"

"Because that's what I was thinking, in those words, when you asked."

"Then we should respond to the call, methinks."

"Yes, we probably ought to find out if we're compatible in that way, too...so we're not distracted while we're trying to work; you know, like wondering?"

Jason gave a nod to the staircase. "Wanna start upstairs?"

Carole laughed throatily and walked over to Jason, dropping her bag on a chair as she passed it. She rubbed her fingertips meaningfully over his shirt. Then she undid the buttons and pulled the front of his shirt out of his jeans. In a husky voice she told him, "No."

Piece o' Cake

"Were you this good when you were alive?" Carole asked him.

Jason chuckled and shook his head.

"Jason, I've been thinking..."

"You've been thinking?" he asked her. "You didn't seem to be thinking."

"I know, I was being thoughtless. What a marvelous respite."

"So you were thinking, and...?"

"What we have here is not incredible, not by Hollywood standards. If it didn't seem so much like *Oh, God* or *Chances Are*, I'd recommend that you turn it into a screenplay." She peered off into the distance where ideas take shape and then returned. "Actually, that's not a bad idea."

Jason smiled at her, "You were thinking," he confirmed.

"Hah! My creative impulses have been at warp speed since you explained this to me. Oh my goodness, was that this morning? What time is it?" She stretched over Jason to check the clock radio display. "Wow, it's four o'clock. We've been procrastinating," she said, attempting to sound like she was chastising him.

"I've never heard it called that."

Carole pulled away, and announcing that she was going to get her computer from downstairs, she slid out of bed. Jason reached out and grabbed her gently by the elbow and then slid his hand down her forearm to her hand where their fingers entwined. He pulled her slowly back toward him. "Not yet," he said, and she slid slowly, and more deliberately back into the bed.

The light was beginning to fade when they resurfaced. They were lying on their backs looking up through a skylight over the bed. Carole spoke first, her tone almost solemn. "I don't know if I ever made love before. I'd like to think I did, if you know what I mean."

"I think we have different descriptions based on where we were at the time. As we evolve, the meanings change by context."

Carole rolled over and kissed his neck and said, "I like that. I feel that all my past sins have been absolved. I've gotten rebaptized."

"You were baptized?"

"Don't get technical with me."

"Ah."

"So may I go get my computer if I promise to hurry back?"

"Huh," Jason said, peering at the woman.

"Huh, you say, and I'm supposed to figure out what that means, right?"

"No. What I'm thinking..."

"Oh, you were thinking?"

"Just a little."

"And what were you thinking about?"

"Dinner."

"That's a good thought," Carole said brightly.

"What would you say to our throwing on some clothes and going downstairs, and I could work on dinner while you work on your computer?"

"Our clothes are downstairs already," she said, offering a perplexed expression which suddenly brightened up, "But we could join them."

"It's a plan."

They climbed out of bed, and without a word of coordination, pulled up the covers, smoothed them and turned them back, and puffed the pillows. Carole looked at Jason. "Don't even think it," she instructed.

"Not I," he insisted and then gestured for her to precede him down the stairs.

"Uh-uh, the man goes first, in case the woman falls."

"Of course," Jason acknowledged and promptly led the way. At the bottom of the staircase he pivoted and she descended into his arms. "You're a very pretty girl," he said,"If that's all right to say."

"It's all right with me...from you...you old coot." They kissed, and sighed, reluctantly parted, gathered up their scattered clothes and got dressed.

Carole perched herself on a stool at a corner of the prep-island while Jason pulled packages from the refrigerator and accoutrements, and cooking vessels from the cupboards. "We're having lamb chops, which I was buying yesterday at TJ's when we met, sort of, for the second time, and roasted string potatoes and broccoli and tomato salad, if that sounds good to you."

"Yummy," Carole responded.

"And how 'bout a nice Sangiovese from Santa Barbara?"

"Jason, I know nothing about wines except whether they taste good, or really good, or not so good."

"That surely is all that matters." He pulled a bottle of White Hawk out from under the prep-island and opened it. "Let's give it a moment or two to breathe, and see if you like it."

"I'm sure I will. I'm not very picky," she said, and then added,"About wines."

"My dear Carole, you are deliciously salacious."

"Why do I think you're not complaining?"

"'Cause I'm not. Now what did you feel was so pressing about getting to your computer?"

"I've had so many new thoughts today, I couldn't have written them all down if I knew shorthand. I thought I would try to start getting them written down."

"Good idea. I won't interrupt. But a quick question first, if I put some music on, would it intrude?"

"Depends on what kind of music. Hip-hop? Rap? Country? Yes, they would intrude."

"I was thinking of Bizet or Prokofiev, or something older. Vivaldi, if that isn't too plebeian."

"Oh, yes, Vivaldi. I love *Winter* if you were thinking of the *Four Seasons*."

"Good choice." Jason walked over to the stereo system, pulled out a CD, inserted it, and told the player which cut he wanted. In a flash the room was filled with Itzhak Perlman giving life to the work of the Red Priest.

Carole stopped keying on her computer and let the music take her. Her eyes were half-closed and her upper body swayed slightly to the remarkable sounds. Jason stopped what he was doing and watched her.

"Hey, aren't you making dinner?" she asked him softly.

"Yeah," he answered, and went back to his preparations. When he had put the chops on the grill and the potatoes in the oven, when the broccoli was in the steamer, and he was about to start on the tomatoes, he was arrested by her critical eye.

"Don't you think the wine has breathed enough?" she asked, with one eyebrow raised.

"Dunno," Jason admitted. "Perhaps I might pour some into glasses and we could see."

"Or taste, as it were," Carole said.

"A better path," Jason agreed and filled two glasses. He then raised his glass toward her. "To a world where we will always appreciate the four seasons."

"Ooh," Carole said, and clinked her glass against his. They sipped. "Ooh, again," she said. "Good choice. It will be perfect with our dinner, too."

She put her glass down and typed a flurry of notes while Jason prepared the tomatoes, then put a flame under the broccoli, and finally flipped the chops. She was still engrossed in entering her notes, and didn't notice Jason then setting the table in the breakfast nook, making it more appropriate for dinner by adding two crystal candle holders and a pair of tapers, and lighting them. When Carole looked up and saw what he had done, she smiled at him. "Very nice touch," she said.

"I'm glad you approve. You deserve the best, for all the work you've been doing...and for who you are." He raised his glass to her again. They clinked again. He refilled their glasses and brought them to the table with the bottle.

There was an indeliberate and mutual shift in focus during dinner. Perhaps like an long-married couple who instead of cooing discussed business. Of course their "marriage" hadn't been long, though they hadn't yet talked about their past lives, so who knew. But their "business" was new and fascinating – "Hi honey, I'm home and have to save the world" – and it was hard to imagine a conversation more intellectually stimulating than about what it would take to shift the consciousness of enough people, and in the right direction; away from disaster and to the next conscious step.

"I think with this issue of consciousness-raising that seeing auras is the key. If we get people to realize that anyone, everyone, can see auras, it will be hard for them to resist. Am I right?" Jason asked Carole.

"Yes," she answered thoughtfully. "The truth is hidden in plain sight but you can't see it unless you are aware. And to be aware, you have to be looking."

"That's right," Jason agreed. "You have to entertain the possibility that auras exist in order to see them."

"Just imagine," Carole confirmed.

"Exactly," Jason said.

"Wow, I think that's a biggie. Now all we have to do is sell the possibility that everyone can do this. No pain, just gain."

"Nice," Jason said. "No wonder they had us hook up. You

are perfect for this."

"Oh, Mr. Isaac, you say the nicest things."

Jason held his glass up toward her, took a sip of his wine and offered, "My bet is that we will want to produce a variety of messages that different people can hear. Some based on opportunity, some on value, some about power."

"Ego, vanity, competition. Don't be left behind, get a leg up on the competition, are you as good as the next guy."

"That's sweet, Carole."

"Well, not sweet, but maybe hitting the sweet spots for different people."

"It's the difference between people who will see a beacon and go to it, and others who will need to have the light shown on them. They have to be searched out and persuaded to follow."

"Do you think maybe that there is just one audience for this, Jason?"

"Meaning?"

"Meaning that people who have attained a certain level of consciousness will know to follow the light, and those who haven't aren't ready to make the shift and, well, they will be left behind. You said that we're five billion people over populated. What do we do about that, call Jenny Craig?"

Jason looked across the table at her thoughtfully. "So this may be a self-selection process?"

"It would maybe simplify things, don't you think?"

"Like the innovators and early adopters. The top thirty per cent, if you will."

Carole clapped her hand to her forehead. "The beacon image

you mentioned. There is another term for early adopter. It is the lighthouse customer. The early adopter will go for the new idea. The middle and late adopters take more time and need to be persuaded."

"Carole, how do you know this stuff?"

She smiled at him. "There is a lot more to advertising than coming up with a slogan to sell a product. You know that. You have to identify your target market, determine the messages that will reach those people, and use the media where they will get those messages."

"I didn't mean..."

"No, no, no, I didn't take it that way," she smiled at him and reached for the wine bottle, refilling Jason's glass first and then her own. "There's a lot of substance in quality advertising. But I guess it's like a lot of things these days, it goes to waste just trying to sell people on buying things they don't need."

"And the beauty of what we are selling is that it is what people need..."

"And only those who realize it will make the purchase, so to say."

"Ooh, yum," said Jason appreciatively. "That makes it easier, doesn't it? The target audience isn't everyone after all. There's no persuading involved."

"Just elucidating."

"Piece o' cake."

A Moment's Paws

With a file in that cake maybe. That's what they were thinking the next morning. And you no doubt felt that after the light speed – in human time – with which they had come together and arrived, safely and sanely, at this amazing juncture, that it would imply some sort of grand wave of momentum that would carry them forward. You'd be in error...for the moment.

"This isn't two-steps-forward-one-step-back is it?" Carole asked over breakfast. "I feel like my brain went for a walk and left the rest of me hanging in the closet."

Jason managed to look at her with a straight face.

Carole laughed. "Okay, well, maybe that's not a complaint. I don't always need my brain. But you know what I mean, don't you?"

"Yes, dear, I do. And if it weren't for an experience I had on my walk just a couple of weeks ago, I might be feeling the same way you are."

"And what, pray tell, Professor Isaac, was that experience?"

"I made a deliberate effort to clear my mind of thoughts and was moderately successful."

"This as opposed to...?"

"Being plagued by thoughts, usually harassing types; what I should be concerned about, where I messed up in the past, or why I was stuck in a piece I was writing, or how to politely get out of an engagement."

Carole looked at him with great interest. "Is that like meditating? Clearing your mind?"

"I suppose so. I was never able to meditate when I tried over the years because I would just try to blank my mind, and all that happened was that thoughts rushed in. Good ones. I had to stop trying to meditate and write them down."

"What did you do differently this time?"

"First, I wasn't sitting down, I was walking, and I think the movement helped. Second, I didn't simply erase the blackboard, as it were, I kept pushing every trace of a thought – about the water, the beach, the sky – out of my mind. And I think it helped that I kept my eyes dancing around – not violently but little tics of movement, every half-second or so I'd guess."

"And it worked?"

"Uh-huh," Jason smiled with humble but excited satisfaction.

"How long did you do it?"

"It was a good 45 seconds, I'd say. I could have gone longer, but I'd achieved what I was trying to do, which was the process. I don't think I could have gone on forever. If the psychologist Julian Jaynes was right, you can only stay in one side of your brain for a maximum of four minutes, and that's with a great deal of practice. Usually it's more like two minutes is tops."

"Which side were you in?"

"Please excuse this side trip, but I really am in awe of how bright you are and how well our thoughts merge."

Carole pretended to look huffy, "Well excuse me, I'm pretty happy with the way the rest of us merges, if you don't mind the interruption, now please continue."

"Hmm," Jason said, a broad smile locking his tongue. After a few seconds his mouth shrank toward normal formation and he could talk again. "My explanation of things is that our right lobe is the receiver of thoughts, ideas, whatever, from the universe and the left lobe is the editor and translator. The left lobe shifts the universal consciousness into terms and images that fit our understanding. The more conscious we are, the less editing there is and the more direct is the translation from the universe to our own awareness. Does that make sense, the way I explained it?"

"Uh-huh," Carole said, "So when you went into that space of no thoughts, where were you?"

Jason looked at her. "I don't know. There was a constant flow of thoughts that I was able to brush off, if you will, but they were small pieces about rocks on the beach or the color of the water, things like that." He thought a moment. "Hmm, good question, I think it must have been the left lobe, because I understood everything. Which makes sense, yes?"

"You're amazing, Jason. I don't know anyone who has delved into their own mind the way you have. And yes, it makes sense."

"Is it important? Is it part of the story we want to tell? Does it help to explain how people can see auras?"

"Oh my goodness, yes, yes, yes. This is what you said last

night to me about metaphor and reason."

"The Robertson Davies line, from *Fifth Business*, yes."

"You said we had to give people both a concept and an example. Like when you give someone directions to some place, and you tell them both the distances in mileage plus you given them landmarks to look for, they can work with ideas and images together."

At that moment, The Dawg entered the picture. Jason put his breakfast plate on the floor for him to lick. "Do you mind sharing, Carole?" he asked, indicating her plate. She took the last piece of bacon from it and put it in her mouth, but as she bit into it, she looked down at The Dawg who was looking at her and she stopped. She took the piece from her mouth and put it back onto the plate. "Excuse me," she said in a syrupy voice, and she put her plate down on the floor next to Jason's.

"He's got a look that would put the average extortionist to shame," she said to Jason.

"You'll learn to manage."

"What does that mean? Not be a victim of his stare?"

"No, you'd never reach that level. Not in this lifetime. You grow to be less bothered by it."

"How 'bout we just cook more?"

The Dawg barked his agreement and then went back to licking the plates.

"He understands English?" Carole asked.

"It's not clear to me if he understands me – and now you – or we understand him. He gets what he wants. And I should add that it rarely conflicts with what I want so it has worked out pretty well."

"He gets inside your head, doesn't he?"

"Yes, when he needs to, but he doesn't do it intrusively. And as I say, it's almost always what I want. Like now, he's ready for his walkie. And it seems like a great time for us, too, don't you think?"

"I think I should give up thinking and leave it to him." Carole reached over and scratched The Dawg behind his ears. "After all, he's done all right by you, or vice versa." She straightened back up. "I'm not intruding, am I?"

The Dawg emitted a not unpleasant whining sound that could only be interpreted as a no.

Carole sighed. "And I thought LA was weird."

"Jason, I was thinking of going over to the other house, where I was house-sitting until two days ago, and, you know, check on things"

"Okay," said Jason, uncertainly. "Are you going to do that now?"

"I guess,"Carole said without enthusiasm.

They walked out of the house together, the three of them. Carole opened her car door, but before she could get in, The Dawg jumped in, parking himself in the passenger's seat.

"Oh," said Carole.

"Uh," Jason wanted to say something but wasn't sure how. "I didn't know if you wanted a break from me, or to be alone, or something, so I didn't ask if I could go with you."

Carole laughed, "I guess The Dawg could read both our minds, since I," her voice broke slightly, "I didn't want to be away from you." She clear her throat. "Is this crazy?" she asked.

"You mean, how we feel about each other? So intense but so

comfortable. So fast, but not hurried?"

"Yeah, like that."

"Dunno. Fits for me."

"Me, too. I just thought I should ask."

She slid into the driver's seat. Jason walked to his own car, pulled a blanket from the trunk and put it on the back seat of her car. "Come on, Dawg," he said, gesturing from him to get out of the front seat. "You get twice as much room in the back." The Dawg complied. Jason said, as he closed the door behind him and got into the passenger's seat, "Plus, I can mess around with the driver."

"Where to?" Carole asked smiling, looking at The Dawg in the rear view mirror. The Dawg arf'd. Carole looked at Jason, "I'm pretty sure he said beach."

"Sounded like that to me," he agreed.

"Good, and we can go to my place later."

"Your place?"

"Well, you know what I mean," she answered plaintively.

"I wonder maybe if you wouldn't feel comfortable moving in with me," Jason said to her softly. "I know it's fast. You can say no. You can say yes and then move out without notice. And I won't charge you rent."

"Huh!" Carole replied jauntily. "I've got that great house on the ridge now. What else are you offering?"

"I'll do the dishes."

"You always did the dishes already."

"Oh yeah," Jason acknowledged. "Um, I'll let you take The Dawg for walks...if I can go with you."

"Okay," Carole relented. She backed the car out of the driveway and headed up the hill toward Route 68. She placed her teeth on her lower lip in the vain attempt to restrain a smile. "It won't take long...going over there. I don't have much. I was just living in a guest room; not making a mess. A suitcase, garment bag and an overnight bag. And the housekeeper is there tomorrow. I should call my friend Joan. I think she will be fine with my going. She was mostly accommodating my need to get away, I think."

"Carole?" Jason said to her in such a strong voice that she pulled over to the side of the street.

"Yes, Jason?"

"I'm so pleased. I didn't know what I was going to do with you not close by."

They leaned toward each other, both with moist eyes, and kissed. When they pulled away, Jason looked into the back seat. "Ya see, that's why I'm in the front seat," he said.

Carole laughed. The Dawg woofed.

Instead of heading west to the ocean, Carole turned east on Route 68 and headed for Highway One, then drove down to the mouth of the Carmel Valley, and quickly back up the aptly-named Outlook Drive. The outlook was towards the top of the ridge, where the view, when the fog was in retreat, was truly spectacular. On a clear day, as the saying goes, one could see for miles and miles; past Pt. Lobos to the south and the mountains beyond Carmel Village to the east.

Carole made a couple of turns and pulled into the driveway of a nondescript but well situated ranch-style house that actually had a lower second level not visible from the street. She got out of the car and stuck her head back in to talk to The Dawg. "No offense, old friend, but if you don't mind staying in the car for a few minutes. There are a couple of old neighborhood cats who spend their days on the deck here, and I don't think they would be interested in entertaining you."

The Dawg didn't say anything. He put his head down on the towel on the seat and just looked at her from under the bottom of his lids. It was as much excitement as Carole knew to expect. She shot him a smile and closed the door. She went around the car and put her hand in Jason's and they walked toward the front door.

"This is where I live...d," she said. "Lived," she repeated as a whole word. "It's so easy to say that now. It makes me so happy about where I'm going to live. And with whom."

She opened the door and, declining Jason's offer of assistance, parked him in a comfortable chair looking out at the view. Over the years he'd been to many parts of the Monterey Peninsula, which had literally hundreds of special places that people could enjoy. This was a new one. His eyes tracked the geography that he had mostly known just from ground level. He traced the road that headed off through the trees toward Big Sur, and another toward Carmel Valley Village, beyond several intervening hills.

In only five minutes, he heard Carole come up behind him. She squeezed his shoulders and then she bent down and moved her hands around him. She squeezed him and said to him softly, "Time to go home, Jason?"

He put his hands over hers and leaned his head back against her. "That's sounds so fine, Carole." It took a little while for them to disentangle, and then Jason stood up.

"I should leave a note for Hannah, the housekeeper," Carole said, walking over to the counter between the dining room and the kitchen.

"Give me the key to the car, and I'll put these in the trunk,"

Jason offered. She tossed him the key.

Two minutes later she had locked up the house and joined him in the car. She chuckled. "The note I left for Hannah, I said that it was a family thing." She twisted in her seat to smile at The Dawg and rub his head. "It is a family, isn't it?"

"Woof," said Jason.

Stretch of Sand

"What do you suppose it is that makes walking by the water so delicious?" Carole asked as she and Jason strolled the expanse of Pacific Ocean beach at the mouth of the Carmel River. They had driven down from Carole's newly-former aerie on the ridge north of Carmel Valley to a spot near Monastery Beach, in the eucalyptus grove by the Bay School.

"I suppose the scientific explanation would be the negative ions." He looked at her. "Know about those?"

She shook her head. "Tell me."

"Well, if I remember what I've read about them, when water is in motion, such as at the seashore, or in a jacuzzi or in the shower or when it rains, an extra electron breaks off from the oxygen molecules and there is a surplus of negative ions. This actually makes you feel better."

"Is that why people put an ionizer in their house or office?"

"That's the idea. I've read that negative ions are much better for you than a heavy concentration of positive ions which you get from the movement of dry air, like the Santa Ana's down where you used to live, or the *foehns* in central Europe or the *zephyrs* in Northern Africa. In Germany, when those winds are blowing, they cancel elective surgeries because the recovery rate is so poor."

"I didn't know what it was, but I've always loved going to the beach. It creates peace inside of me."

"The less scientific explanation might be that we are mostly salt water. Hence the attraction."

"Hence indeed," she told him. They walked in silence for several minutes. "Do you think it's really possible that we are witnessing this shift in consciousness, that it's going to be happening now?"

"Our mission impossible?"

"That's the one. It seems rather enormous, but it also seems time. Doesn't it, or am I just a silly girl?"

Jason stopped and brought them together. "You are so far from silly, my dear, the word has no business in your lexicon."

"That's a sweet thing to say, though I'm not sure everyone would think so."

"Vocabulary is the key to a woman's heart," Jason intoned.

"Who said that, Noah Webster?" Carole asked, laughing.

Jason grinned. "Musta been."

"But I'm a little concerned that not everyone is going to be happy to learn about auras, and what they mean. I was in a little bakery in Santa Barbara a few years ago, and there was a woman with a maybe six-month old in a baby carriage. When I looked at the child, I could see such wisdom, such light. I leaned over a little toward the baby and said something like, 'Hello there, you're an old soul, aren't you?' And the baby's face just lit up and started gurgling and waving her arms about." Carole chuckled.

"Really?"

"The mother went crazy. She screamed, I don't know what, and wheeled the baby out of the bakery as fast as she could. Obviously she'd never seen her behave that way."

"Maybe she thought you were a witch, of some sort," Jason offered.

"I was Glinda, The Good Witch of the North."

"Glinda was from the south."

"I was her twin sister, Glinda."

"Like Larry, Darryl, and Darryl."

"Oh silly boy, we went by auras not names."

"Except when people dropped in from Kansas."

"*Exactement!*"

"The baby saw that I saw her. It must have been the first time she had been recognized," Carole said with a laugh, "I'm sorry I scared the mother, but it's like seeing auras, don't you think?"

"Yes, and you're right. Learning about it is going to scare some people out of their wits. I was talking with Tony Seton, the fellow who's doing the video on auras, and he agrees that babies can see auras but they're taught not to. The parents saying, 'There isn't that color around that man,' or 'It's just your imagination,' and that sort of thing. But I think before they stop seeing them, it's peoples' auras that some-times cause infants to react loudly against them. They can see the negativity in someone, see that they are dangerous or unhealthy or something."

Jason was thoughtful as he continued, "But you know, while

there will be people who will freak out like that mother, there will be a significant number of people who will embrace it."

"Like the innovators and the early adopters?"

"Precisely that. I was on my daily perambulation when a couple, probably in their mid-forties, asked me to take their picture, which of course I did. And then we got to talking and they told me with pride and awe about their son. They said that Ethan, from the time he was maybe eighteen months old, but before he had really learned to talk, he was fascinated with bridges. He would point upward when they drove under one, really excited.

"And then as he grew older he was avid about becoming an architect, and especially for designing bridges. He announced that he was headed to MIT at age seven, they said.

"But what was most fascinating to me was that when I asked them if they understood how this was possible – I asked if they were religious, and she wasn't and he didn't seem zealous – the mother said sort of quietly, that she thought that he had had a past life. Of course that seemed like the only plausible explanation. There really isn't another one, is there?"

"That's such a wonderful story, Jason. I wonder how many other parents have brilliant children – prodigies, I guess they'd be called – if they were allowed and encouraged to flourish."

Carole was decided. "You're right, Jason, we have to think about it from that perspective. About how when people find out, it will be good for them."

"I've been thinking that for all too long we've been like the public schools, always dumbing down classes to the slowest students, instead of focusing on the brightest children and nourishing their minds. I think it's the biggest problem in our society that we don't hold ourselves to higher standards. Push people to raise themselves."

"I had a friend who loved to quote *Democracy in America*. He said de Tocqueville noted a characteristic of Americans that they were less likely to try to achieve more than they were to pull their betters down."

"I remember that," Jason said. "It's so true. You look at the tea party and the faux conservatives. They're not about making America better. They retard us, and when they hold us back, they hold back the world."

"You think that, that America is a leader for the rest of the world."

"I do. I think we are the synthesis of the East and the West. That we have the capacity to break through to the next step."

"And what is that?"

"Peace, I think. Just imagine what would be possible if we stopped funding our militaries. If all the nations worked together to end piracy and terrorism. We could wipe it out in months. Use financial pressures to get the slow learners into line."

"Jason," said Carole, stopping and moving up against him, putting her arms around him, her head on his chest, holding him tightly. "That's what seeing auras can do." She pulled her head back, looked fiercely into his eyes and said, "Will do."

"Will do, Carole."

They walked on and soon reached the mouth of the Carmel River where they climbed a small knoll, at the top of which was a large wooden cross. Jason stood with his back against it and pulled Carole back against him so they could both look out at Point Lobos and the ocean. For a minute they just looked out at the view. Then Jason told her about the cross.

"It was said that this was where one of the earliest Spanish explorers landed and erected a cross so that other ships would see it and stop and bring them provisions. It's not clear what happened to them – we're talkin' four centuries ago – but over the years the cross has always been here."

"The original one?" Carole asked, pulling away and turning to take a look at the fifteen-foot cross made of rough-hewn eight-by-eights.

"No, it's been replaced a bunch of times, I guess when the wood rotted." Jason chuckled. "The last time was maybe in the Sixties. I think some chuckle-heads burned down the cross, and if the story is right, all sorts of political haranguing went on, with county and local officials arguing about who or which agency had jurisdiction, and some ACLU types getting into the action and claiming that there shouldn't be a cross there at all. Religious freedom, I think."

"How absurd," Carole said with an infrequent frown furrowing her forehead. "The cross isn't a religious symbol, not always. It's a marker. A point of intersection. What nonsense." Then she smiled. "I guess they didn't win."

"No, they didn't. According to local lore, in the middle of the night, some guys came up from Big Sur and put up a new cross using old timber."

"Ooh, I like that," Carole said. "The people and common sense winning one." She took Jason's hands. "Come on, let's go home."

"I like the sound of that so much, Carole," Jason said. He pushed away from the cross and then, still holding her hands, pulled his hands behind him, drawing her to him. Their lips met.

Soon they were on the way to the house. Jason diverted Carole to a new restaurant in Carmel called Pastries and Petals. It was in a courtyard away from the center of town. "When," Carole wondered aloud, "will they start being more business-friendly in this town and let people put up signs so new customers can find their stores."

"They could also add street numbers," Jason agreed.

Carole shook her head. "There are limits to how quaint is quaint," she said. "And yet it's such a charming town."

They got out of the car and with The Dawg sat at an empty table on the patio. A woman came out of the store with a big smile on her face. "Jason, it's been too long. " He got up and they embraced.

"Carole, this is Jeanne. Jeanne, Carole."

The woman looked at Carole for a few seconds, and then back at Jason. "Oh my, I think you've found her, haven't you?"

Jason raised his eyebrows,"Yep. Sorry. I guess it's over between us, Jeanne."

"I'll muddle through, I guess," Jeanne said, smiling and feigning disappointment. She looked at Carole. "I'm delighted for you, I truly am. Jason hasn't been as happy as he could be," she looked at him again, "until now. Oh, I'm so pleased. Lunch is my treat."

Jason started to protest. "Hush, you," Jeanne said. "I'll be back with menus."

"Am I really having that kind of effect? Is it so visible?"

"It must be."

Jeanne was back quickly with the menus which she handed first to Carole and then to Jason. She also had brought out a ham bone that she gave to The Dawg.

She laughed at the pleasure on The Dawg's face. "He knows I treat him right."

Over a delicious luncheon of curried chicken salad and Panini with Gruyere and smoked ham and a bottle of Bernardus 2009 Chardonnay, Carole and Jason relaxed, more as a couple than they had ever been. It was not long before they were on a variation on the theme that had brought them together – telling the world about auras.

"Maybe you should be the frontman – or woman – for this enterprise," Jason suggested.

Carole shook her head slowly and didn't stop, but she was also smiling.

"What no?" Jason persisted, trying not to smile back. "I mean after all, you're bright, personable, witty, and certainly attractive."

Carole just sat looking at him over her glass of wine, not saying anything.

"All right, all right, I've got it." He raised his eyebrows a couple of times quickly to make his point, "We would do a great dog-'n-pony. Which do you want to be?" He stopped and looked closely at her. "Are you allowed to ask a woman that?"

"Certainly not," Carole responded with fake horror which then immediately dissipated into laughter. "Besides, we've already got The Dawg, and I've never been much with the horsey set. I'll hold up the applause sign."

Jason chuckled. "Sounds like a cushy job to me. You too?" he asked as he reached down and rubbed The Dawg's head. The Dawg didn't even look up as he gnawed at the bone. "He thinks so, too," he reported to Carole.

It was then that Jeanne came back with a tray of a half-dozen small cakes. "Sweets for the sweets," she announced proudly, pointing at "carrot cake, devil's food, lemon, chocolate, vanilla, and spice."

"Oh my goodness," Carole said, "where are we supposed to put those? I haven't eaten so much for lunch since I was a fat child."

Jeanne looked at her. "You were fat?"

Carole nodded. "When I was eight. I was confused. I thought I was growing up, but I was just adding weight. Of course at that age I could take it off quickly, but I never got rid of the memory of feeling fat."

"Aha, well then, I'll put them in a box for you. You can enjoy them when you have more room. Okay?"

"Delighted," came Carole's reply. "Thank you. And thank you for a delicious lunch."

"And I'll bring a box for The Dawg to bring his bone in, if you can get it away from him for the ride."

The Dawg looked up at her, the bone between his paws. Jeanne could have sworn that he smiled.

PSR

Upon their return to the house, Jason made room in his closets and bureau for Carole to put her clothes away. He also cleaned out several drawers in the bathroom cabinet, and provided her with extras towels and whatever he could imagine she might need. Carole protested mildly, pointing out that she didn't have much with her, but warning that when she would move her things up from Los Angeles, there wouldn't be enough room for any of his things.

As she finished her unpacking, she turned to find Jason holding out to her a glass of champagne. She took the glass and held it out to Jason.

"To our life together," he said, his voice breaking. Carole's eye glistened.

"To our wonderful life together," she said softly. They clinked glasses and sipped. "Yum. I love champagne."

"Of course it's not real champagne," Jason said in his best pontificating voice," because the French are pretty snooty about the fact that to be called such it has to be from their Champagne region, but, hey, we're making some nice bubbly here in California."

"Is this the split of Roderer I saw in your fridge?"

"Our fridge, Miz Holley."

"Our fridge, Mr. Isaac. Thank you." They toasted again.

The phone rang. Jason answered it. Carole watched him through a short conversation. "Hi." "Sure." "Great." "See you then."

Jason disconnected the call and told her, "Tony Seton is in town. He wants to get together to talk about The Professor. He suggested that we meet at Spanish Bay around 5:30 this afternoon. We can sit on the patio and enjoy the sunset if the fog doesn't interfere."

"Oh goodie. And they have a bagpiper there, don't they? I think Joan told me."

"That's right," Jason smiled. He checked his watch. "Two hours," he announced. "We have time for a nap."

"What a good idea."

Five-thirty found them sitting around a fire pit outside at Spanish Bay. Tony was already there. He rose to greet them and then signaled a waitress who brought blankets and menus. The fog had seemed to thicken in just the few minutes they were there, but the wind had abated so it wasn't terribly cold. Still, Carole and Jason joined Tony in Irish coffees.

"I'm glad you were free on short notice," he told them. "I wanted to arrange a trip for you up to Mendocino to see The Professor. Some friends who have been working with him have a Cessna Skylane, if you don't mind small planes."

Jason looked at Carole who shook her head. "Fine with us. When would that be?"

"Day after tomorrow, if that works for you. I don't know how flexible are your schedules."

"Flexible," Jason said, with Carole's nod of agreement.

"Great. I'll confirm with Geoffrey," Tony said. "I think you know them, don't you? Geoffrey Lucerne and Ariane Chevasse?"

"They were the ones who revealed that the oil industry was sitting on key solar developments, I think," Jason said. "He was an anchorman with a Sacramento station, and she was the daughter of the physicist who actually broke the story to Geoffrey?"

"That's right. And they moved down to Monterey right after that. Actually, they're in Pacific Grove," Tony pointed his head north. "Over by the dunes."

"Nice spot," Jason said.

"Except for the fog," Tony noted. "Anyway, they hooked up with The Professor and have been working with him on how to get his discovery out."

"What are they thinking?"

Tony smiled at them. "I think I'll let them tell you, if you don't mind. Mostly because I'm not sure where they are in the planning." He paused and then added, "I don't mean to sound hush-hush..."

"No, of course, that's fine," said Jason. "I think I might have met them at some event around here. I don't remember which. Very substantial-looking."

Tony cocked his head at Jason. "Yes. Yes, they are very substantial. She has her own interesting background, which again I'll let her share with you." He laughed. "I sound like we're in a James Bond movie."

Carole asked, "Tony, what is your role in all of this?"

"I thought I was going to write a book for The Professor in which he would explain the PSR process." He stopped himself. "Do you know about that?"

Jason waggled his head. Carole shook hers.

"That's why I wanted to get together with you," he said. "The Professor is a strange duck, as you might imagine. A physicist working alone in a basement lab on the Mendocino Coast on a discovery...Well, I'm getting ahead of myself a bit. First, I wanted to tell you that you'll have probably an hour or so with him. That's all he really wants to spend away from his work, especially at this stage. It's in its final development."

"Are you going to write his book?" Carole asked.

"No, actually. We decided that it would leave out too many people. I suggested that he explain the process on tape. I would shoot him using a blackboard and then insert visuals over it to make it more accessible to more people. He agreed. I finished the taping last weekend and am now cleaning it up in post-production. I've cut it down to about nine and a half minutes, so I can put it up on *YouTube*."

Tony laughed again. "He is the perfect caricature of the Sam Jaffe scientist in *The Day the Earth Stood Still*. Not the same body type, but the same busy academic style. And The Professor was particularly busy trying to shoehorn eleven minutes of copy into a nine-minute format. I have him wearing a white lab coat and standing, as I said, in front of a blackboard. He was surprisingly good. He always seemed to me that he would be more comfortable talking to a crowd of physicists, but he was able to translate what he has done to a level that most high schoolers should be able to understand."

"That's terrific," Jason said.

"A former TV news guy, you can appreciate that he comes off better at the blackboard than most corporate types would with a PowerPoint presentation. He's very human. That's what clinches it. The only people who will doubt him, or challenge him, will do so because they don't want to believe him. So be it. Like the climate change deniers."

He hunched forward. "I wanted to explain to you about PSR before you met The Professor. He will be pleased that he doesn't have to go through it from scratch."

"PSR?" Carole asked.

"Parallel Spectographic Recoloration. It's a process The Professor designed. What it does is it makes the human aura visible to the human eye."

Carole looked at Jason who nodded his head. "I heard a little about this," he told her, "but not the details."

"The big piece," Tony continued after a measured glance around, "is that he has not only made it visible but he has devised a set of algorithms that enable the viewer to assess the character of the person of whose aura he's looking at. I explained this sketchily to Jason last week, and since then the software has been tweaked and it really is amazing. It's everything a polygraph can do, but much more accurate. There is no room for doubt about its accuracy."

"What does it measure, exactly?" Jason asked.

"It measures consciousness according to three axes that wind up displaying in the aura as lumens, chroma, and hue. Hue is the shade of a color, the lumens is the thickness of the light as in solid or degree of translucence, and chroma is the brightness of the color. I know that sounds a little confusing, but when you see it on the monitor it will become more obvious.

"The three variables register the level of a person's consciousness in terms of their overall awareness; that's the hue. It's more than how much they know but more like their wisdom. How they've integrated their knowledge into understanding. The closer the hue is to indigo, the higher the consciousness.

"The lumens references the quality of the consciousness. What they are doing with it. There are some people who know what's going on but don't use it properly. They've decided to exploit their awareness. The higher the lumens quotient, the more solid the color is – the closer to solid – the more they are invested in their consciousness for noble purpose; you expect more integrity. If their color is thinner, they aren't committed, you might say."

He paused there and got nods of understanding from his rapt audience of two. "And chroma tells you where the person resides in terms of the moment. Are they focused on the past, the future, or are they present? A color that is so bright that it starts to bleed indicates a person who is thinking about the future. At the other end of the spectrum, a person who has a very low level of color – think about adjusting the color level on a monitor and it heads toward black-'n-white – that's a low chroma, and it says the person is stuck in the past, that they are trapped by where they have been. But when the color is pure, it says that the person is living in the here and now and is more balanced." He looked at them again. "Does that make sense? I know I'm just giving you an outline."

"Do you have any examples?" Carole wondered.

"Yes, of course. Good," Tony said. "Let's talk about people we all know, or think we do. Bill Clinton, for example. He would be in the green-blue area because he's pretty bright, but the depth of the color hasn't been consistently strong. Probably because of his upbringing, he never really committed himself to doing the right thing. He's mostly just about himself."

"And his chroma?" asked Carole.

"He has a high chroma level," Tony acknowledged with a wry smile, "which is interesting because in a sense he's stuck in the past and trying to escape it. But his mind is on what's next. Often, regrettably, in terms of which women he can charm into bed. He's always on a quest that way."

"So his color is blue-green, or green-blue," said Jason, "it's not a solid color, and it tends to be overly-bright. Is that right?"

"Yes, very good."

"Another example, please," Carole requested. "How about Meryl Streep?"

Tony smiled at her. "Interesting choice. I haven't seen her in the PSR system, but from what I've read about her, my guess is that she is a thick blue, as The Professor would describe a solid color, and when she's not acting, I'm thinking she might be a tad low on the chroma. I think that's true with many in the profession, even when they are at the top, because they're often thinking of their last game or their last performance and picking nits about how they did."

"That would makes sense," Carole said, "especially since she is a perfectionist, at least that's what I heard."

"How 'bout Khaddafi?" Jason asked.

"Glad you mentioned him," Tony replied, "because there is another factor in the PSR formula. It has to do with the amount of change that is going on in a person. At the edge of the aura, away from the body, is what The Professor refers to as the corona. It charts the stability of the consciousness. You might think about the outside edge of the sun, when

87

you're looking at a solar eclipse. The smoother the edge, the more consistent the character. If there's a lot of spurting and crackling, like solar flares, it's an indication of instability. If it's really ragged – you know, like static displaying on a monitor – then it's an indication of real craziness. But if it's just a little edgy, it's usually a sign of transition, and that's usually growth."

"Fascinating," Jason commented with enthusiasm,"Absolutely fascinating. You gave me a taste of this before, but getting into it more is fascinating."

"You didn't know about this?" Carole asked him.

Jason shook his head. "Not the details. It seems so obvious, though, doesn't it?"

"I'd like to see it in action," Carole told him. "I think putting the visual in front of me would help a lot. But I get the theory."

"Good," said Tony. "I know this is complicated, and you're right, when you see The Professor take people through the PSR software, you will know right away how logical it is."

"What about Khaddafi?" she asked.

Tony took a breath. "He's a piece of work, as you know. His aura is a thin reddish-black color. His chroma vacillates between very high highs and very low lows. He's quite schizophrenic and never dealing with reality, which is in the now."

"And let me guess about his corona?" Carole said. "It's all crackly."

"Like a sun storm," Tony confirmed. "The Professor said he hadn't seen many coronas that wild. It makes sense, of course."

"Indeed it does," Jason agreed. "There are few people in

public life who seem as whacky as he does."

Carole asked, "What's your aura like, Tony? If I can ask?"

He laughed. "I suspect it's pretty much likes yours," he said. "Blue, thick, even chroma. A smooth corona, though maybe a little simmering. The learning curve has been high, and incorporating what I've been finding out into my existing self has been interesting. I think fascinating was the word you used."

"Well, Jason could see auras after he came back. He said mine was blue and thick, I think he used that word. But I couldn't see his. I don't think. I mean, when I look at him, I see his energy. Or at least I feel that I do. It feels bright and healthy and, and, I was going to say pretty but that doesn't sound right. Attractive, I guess."

"Came back?" Tony asked.

Carole looked quickly at Jason. "Oops?"

Jason smiled at her. "No, Carole. No oops." He turned to Tony. "This may sound weird to you, but then again, it may not." He proceeded to tell him the story of his "death". He was pleased to see that the man's expression didn't change.

When it was his turn to respond, he first said to Carole, "No, Carole. No oops." The relief on her face was obvious. Then to both of them, "I've read too much, heard too much, and seen for myself too much to find your account even surprising. Interesting, yes, especially with what you were told. But when you consider that some 25 million people who have had near-death experiences describe seeing the same thing, then I have to think that there is something going on. I refer to it as the larger reality. I know it exists even if I don't know what it is."

"I like that...larger reality," said Jason. "May I borrow it?"

Tony laughed. "Be my guest," he said. Then to Carole, "You'll be able to see your auras up at The Professor's lab. He has a camera that feeds into the computer. The image is live."

"With the PSR?"

"Yes."

"Oh how neat. I can't wait to see what you really look like Jason."

"I hope you still like me," Jason said with a faux pout.

"Well yeah, after our move today. It would be embarrassing to have to call Joan again after two days," Carole harrumphed with a laugh. "Tony, what were your thoughts when you saw this working?"

"Funny you should ask that," he replied. "Part of me was amazed at what I was seeing. And another part of me was awed by what it meant. I mean, this is going to change everything."

Twixt Heaven and Earth

Tony said he would call in the morning to confirm the flight the following day to Mendocino. As they drove back up to their house, Jason asked Carole what she thought of him. "He's very bright, of course, like you." She peered at Jason. "But he's not as cute as you are."

"You're prejudiced."

"Am not!"

"You're not?"

"Well, maybe."

"All right then."

"Didn't you like him, too?"

"I did. I do. He's a man of substance. No wonder we all have the same type of aura."

Carole giggled.

"What's funny?"

"That we're talking in these terms. I mean, consider that we

91

weren't speaking this way only a couple of weeks ago, and now it's an important part of what we know. Hugely important."

"That's putting it mildly."

"I didn't want to ruffle my corona," Carole replied, trying to keep a straight face.

"I'd love you anyway."

"Even if I was just a common flower girl?" replied Carole in her best Liza Doolittle.

"What kind of flowers?"

Carole couldn't contain her laughter anymore. They had just pulled into the driveway, and she threw her arms over Jason. "We're home, my darling."

As they got out of the car, The Dawg circled round from the back of the house, his tail wagging. "Hi, Dawg," Carole cried, and his tail wagged faster. She walked over to him, bent over and rubbed his face. "We missed you. It was a business meeting at Spanish Bay and they don't seem to like your type on the patio. Sorry. Their loss."

Jason had opened the door for them and The Dawg led Carole, with the doorman following. Carole turned and closed on Jason who put his arms around her. Speaking into his chest she asked, "Jason?"

"Yes, Carole," he replied in stentorian tones.

"Is it all right that I want to hold you so much?"

"Yes, Carole," he repeated.

"And you feel the same way about me?"

"At least."

"Mmm, that's good."

"Yes, Carole."

"Jason?"

"Yes, Carole."

"You won't get tired of saying that will you?"

"No, Carole."

"Good." She sighed and pulled her head back and looked up at him. "I had more alcohol than I'm used to. Maybe I should make us some coffee?"

"Okay," Jason said, "but not yet." And he gently placed her head back against his chest.

That's when they heard six distinct bell tones. "What's that?" Carole asked.

"I don't know," Jason told her. "It sounded like the bells on the old news wire machines back forty years ago when there was a new bulletin."

"It came from your office."

"Yes it did."

They separated and walked tentatively up the stairs to the office and stopped in the doorway. At that moment the computer screen came on. "Oh," said Jason as suddenly there was an image filling the screen. Two women and a man sitting in what looked like a conversation area in maybe the Red Carpet lounge at O'Hare Airport.

"Is that...?" Carole asked as Jason pulled a chair from a corner and put it next to his own. They sat down next to each other in front of the monitor.

"Yep."

The picture vanished, but it was clear that the screen was still active. Jason pulled the keyboard toward him and at typed, "Is that you, Klaatu?"

Very, very slowly letters appeared on the screen that finally spelled, "Yes, Jason. It is I."

Jason typed, "My god, you type slowly."

The responding letters came back a little more quickly. "Our god, Jason. And speed is not everything, as you know."

Carole asked Jason. "Is it all right if I join you?"

Instantly the word "Sure" filled the screen.

Carole slid herself closer to Jason and rested her hand on his thigh; he put his hand atop hers. In that moment the word disappeared from the screen and they were looking again at the scene from heaven. Jason told Carole, "That's it, the airport lounge." As if on cue, the shot slowly zoomed in on the three people. "That's they," he said, pointing to them on the screen. "That's Klaatu, SueLan, and Sinead."

Carole whispered to Jason, "They're exactly as you described them. And the place. Oh my..."

"Welcome to you, Carole," Klaatu said with a warm smile. "You did so well to link up with our Jason so quickly."

"Your Jason?" she questioned, her voice loud with possession. "Not anymore. Not ever again."

Jason chuckled.

Klaatu quickly clarified, "No, please, I didn't mean it that way. Be assured that he is not coming back here."

"That's right," Sinead said, "You can keep him."

"All right then," Carole said, relieved and amused, but trying not to show it. Later she would tell Jason she felt like she had been dropped into an audition for a sitcom.

"All right then," repeated Klaatu. "You had a good meeting

with Tony Seton."

"Are they always watching us?" Carole asked Jason aghast.

Sinead answered her, "We could but we don't. Unless it's something urgent, but it never is."

"Phew," she said to Jason. "That's a relief."

"Yes," Jason responded. "He filled us in..." He stopped and then restarted. "I guess you know all of that."

"Yes, of course," Klaatu answered evenly. "We wanted to check in with you, to let you know that we are monitoring your progress. You connection with Carole was most timely."

"Uh-huh."

"We wanted to let you know..." Klaatu began, but then SueLan interrupted him. "We didn't want you to worry."

"About what?" Jason asked, worried.

"That we were watching you," Klaatu told them. "Also that you will find that your ability to see auras is going to fade."

"Why? I thought that's what this was all about. Saving the Earth by telling people how they could see them."

Carole squeezed his leg gently.

"It was and it is. The process of expanding consciousness is a bit complicated. That's why we wanted to speak to you now."

"All ears, gang," Jason told them.

"First, we connected you with Carole, as I think you probably surmised, so that she would be able to remind you of where you've been. And we will not be out of contact with you, so you have no need to worry about that."

"So I was just supposed to see auras for a few days?"

"That's right. You need to understand that seeing auras is no great trick. Everyone born on the Earth can do it. Babies see auras, but their parents teach that out of them as you have already surmised. After a while, the babies stop seeing them because their reality is denied. It's part of their acclimatizing to society on Earth."

SueLan chimed in, "Most people in your insane asylums are there because they could always see auras, and they couldn't accept that other people didn't."

Carole coughed lightly; it was a staged sound that Jason smiled at but its effect was lost on those upstairs.

Sinead put in, "The next step in your evolution is actually a step back. To recover your innate human ability to see auras. That will cause a massive upheaval on the planet during which you will move to the next step, which is instead of seeing auras you will read people's energy through the third eye. You know about the third eye, don't you?" There was the slightest hint of condescension in her tone.

"I do," Carole said preempting Jason who she knew was likely to throw her a *bon mot* of his own.

Jason patted her hand and reported, "There have been a number of higher cultures in the past that actually broke a hole in the forehead so that special members of their tribe could see through it more easily. Those who survived the operation." His tone was dry.

Having seen sparks fly between the two at their first meeting, Klaatu moved to regain control. "Yes, well, the next step will be to see without seeing, if you will, but for now the issue is auras, and your role in spreading the word is vital to jump-starting the process." He turned to SueLan. "That's the right term, isn't it?"

"Yes, Klaatu," she said to him fondly.

"Oy," said Sinead, "Here's the thing, you two. There have been some, uh, unforeseen circumstances...."

"Why don't I like the sound of that?" Jason shot at her.

"Maybe because I said it," Sinead retorted, and she wasn't wrong. "Anyway, listen up. You'll be fine. In fact you've gotten a great deal, but you need to stay on your fingers."

Carole and Jason looked at each other. Jason asked her, "Do you means toes? Stay on our toes?"

Sinead looked annoyed, with herself. "Fingers, toes...they're all digits."

Klaatu cleared his throat. "Yes, well, you must be alert. There are some players on the stage who will not be pleased with your efforts. You need to understand that they don't want people to be able to see auras. They don't want that very badly. It will mean massive financial losses to them."

"They don't sound very conscious," Carole observed.

"No," said SueLan with something of a shudder. "They're in the red-black area. Their chroma levels are extreme in both directions. Depressive types with dangerous grabs for a future that meets their needs. We refer to them as emotional epileptics."

"We think we will keep them away from you," Klaatu said, trying to sound reassuring.

"That would probably be a good idea," Jason agreed. "And just so there's no confusion here, if I ever feel that Carole is in any danger whatsoever, we'll be out of your sandbox faster than you can say Jack Robinson."

"Ditto for me about Jason," Carole told them firmly.

There was silence on the other end of the conversation.

Finally SueLan spoke. "Excuse us, but who is this Jack Robinson and why would we be saying his name?"

Jason chuckled. "Not to worry," he told them. "It's just an expression meant to signify high speed."

"Ahso," said Klaatu. "Thank you for the clarification. And the sandbox reference we understood, yes. Thank you. But no, you won't have to leave. Your role is integral, both of you, and you will play it. And you will not become a target of the primitives."

"I wish I could be as certain as you. No offense."

"None taken, Jason. I can appreciate from your perspective that this is a – how do you say, dicey – time. Nature is not nice, not compassionate. She's efficient. Man is the only species that has refused to work with Her."

"Was that meant to be encouraging?" Carole asked Jason.

Jason raised his eyebrows.

"I see your point, Miss Holley," Klaatu said.

"What is your role in it, then?" she asked him directly. "I mean, here are we, apparently at the mercy of an unhappy Mother Nature about to clean up our mess. Are you just observers, or do you have actual powers to intervene?"

"It's not as simple as that," Sinead told her in a clipped tone.

Carole was having none of her attitude. "I'm not simple either. Perhaps you would explain it to me."

"Well we are not God, you know. We don't have the power to part the seas or rain locusts down on certain countries."

"What can you do?"

"We are observers, Miss Holley," said SueLan, "But sometimes we can intervene. Moving the pieces on the chessboard a space or two sometimes, to get them in the way or out of the way, so that it benefits people."

"And do you have a broader purpose?"

"Well of course," Sinead jumped back in, a tad testily. "We are trying to raise the consciousness of Earth so it can move forward." She said to Klaatu, "I thought we had made all this clear to her boyfriend."

"Uh, he told me what you had said, but from what he told me and from what I've learned from listening to you myself now, I can't say you generate a lot of confidence."

Sinead tried to interrupt but Carole rode right over her. "This isn't a game for us. We are alive. We like our lives. We want to continue them, and be productive. You can understand, surely, that we don't want to be backhanded by conflicting forces over which we have no control, and which don't have much invested in our survival."

Jason added, "We don't want to wind up as collateral damage in some failed experiment." He paused and then added, "I think you can understand that."

The three sat quietly. The Earth people's message had gotten through. Klaatu cleared his throat. "You have made your point expertly. You have shown us that not only did we pick the right person..."

"The right people," SueLan noted quickly.

"Yes," Klaatu corrected himself, "Of course, the right people. Excuse me, Miss Holley."

Carole nodded.

"And when I say that," Klaatu continued, "I mean not only that are you right for this task we have given you, but you are even more up to it than we imagined."

SueLan said, "You have raised the bar of our expectations is what Klaatu is saying."

Carole smiled wryly at Jason. "I guess that's supposed to be comforting," she said.

Jason wore an expression she couldn't quite assess but decided to wait until after their conference with the heavenly beings to ask him about it. Jason for his part was about done with the conversation and was about to sign off when a question occurred to him.

"Could I ask, is our time with you when we're down here like it would be if we were up there? I mean, will it have been just a fraction of a second that has passed here when we finish?"

"As a matter of fact that's correct," said Klaatu. "You are on our clock, as it were. Heaven does lots of interventions, and so what amounts to a fraction of a second delay on Earth mounts up, and we have to adjust the terrestrial time references every so often so it doesn't get out of synch with the rest of the universe. That's why every four cycles is Leap Year."

Carole said to Jason, "You know, that's the only explanation that has ever really made sense to me. For what it's worth," she added.

Klaatu bestowed on them a beatific smile. "I'm glad we're ending this conversation on an upbeat note. I expect we will talk again soon."

Winging North

The telephone had rung at nine o'clock, almost exactly, Jason had noted. "I like that kind of precision," he told Carole after he'd gotten off the call with Tony. "He said we should be at Monterey Bay Aviation tomorrow morning at ten. If there's fog, it should have burned off by then. If not, it doesn't matter because Geoffrey is instrument rated, and it's his plane."

"You said that you knew him and...what's her name?"

"Ariane. Ariane Chevasse. Geoffrey met her father who was a physicist who'd been involved with major solar break-throughs. The fellow died shortly thereafter and Geoffrey hooked up with his daughter, who happened to be very bright. A spook, I think?"

"A spook?"

Jason laughed, "Yes, a sort of spy. Into cybernetics and cryptography, that kind of stuff."

"Uh-huh," Carole responded.

"Anyway, Geoffrey and Ariane blew the top off the story

that the oil importers association was sitting on these dis-coveries. And in the course of it all fell madly in love."

"Sounds somewhat familiar, doesn't it?" Carole asked as she sat down on Jason's lap. She kissed him long and soft.

"Ya think?" he teased her when they finally got their lips separated. "Not just another workplace romance?"

"I wouldn't know about that. You said he was an anchorman in Sacramento?"

Jason chuckled. "Yes, he was. He was fired for breaking the story, even though it wasn't done intentionally. When he went public with the story of his being fired, the company that owned the station where he had been the top ratings earner in the market canned the station manager who had fired him, and wound up paying him a ton of money. They moved down here right after the story broke, and I'm not sure what they've been doing since. Some entrepreneur stuff I think but I'm not sure." Then he remembered, "She's close friends with Francie, who was at Cindy's party."

"Oh yes, I remember her. Nice lady. Smart, classy. Of course it's amazing that I remember anyone there since I spent almost every second with you."

"Was there anyone else there?" He pulled her face down to his again. Their passion, though gentle, spoke of primal need, and pure pleasure.

"Do you think we'll ever get tired of this?" Carole asked, her breath ragged.

"Not in this lifetime," Jason answered and kissed her again.

"So, um, where was I?"

Jason thought for a moment. "You asked if I knew Geoffrey and Ariane. I don't know them really. I think we've been at a couple of the same events. I might have been introduced to him, but if we spoke, it was only briefly. I saw her, as I remember, but we didn't actually meet. Still I had a sense that they were good people."

"That doesn't surprise me, considering what's going on in our lives together, that we should be meeting good people. I like this...a lot. I bet we like them, too."

The next morning they arrived at the airport a few minutes before ten and stood outside the lounge, looking out over the ramp and across the field. Jason spied Geoffrey moving about a Cessna 182. He'd flown enough in small planes to know that he was pre-flighting the aircraft, making sure that everything was in order.

"Jason, right?" The voice came from a woman he quickly recognized. She was walking across the adjacent open hangar toward them. "*Bon jour*, Jason. I have seen you, I think," she said in a delicious French accent. She shook he hand. "I am Ariane Chevasse. And you must be Carole. *Enchantée*." She leaned forward and kissed her on both cheeks. Medium height with dark auburn hair that turned up as it reached her shoulders, her face was slightly tan and she had dark blue eyes that saw a lot. She had considerable presence, though not at all intrusive.

"Come," she said, leading them across the tarmac, "I'm sure that Geoffrey is done with his pre-flighting of *Avionne*."

"*Avionne*," said Carole, "and Ariane? Any connection?"

Ariane laughed, "You know there might have been, but Geoffrey named her before he met me. Still, it is *très intéressant* since he made the name out of the French word for plane which is *avion*. He added an *n* and an *e*. And I think you might have guessed that I am French, too. Well, I'm American, but my roots are French."

"*Bienvenue*," Jason intoned.

"*Ca c'est bien!*" Ariane responded with a welcoming smile. They arrived at the aircraft. "Geoffrey, I think you know Jason, and this is Carole."

Geoffrey was an attractive six-footer with short but combable dirty blond hair that framed a boyish, rectangular face that sported a natural year-round tan. He smiled warmly and shook their hands. "I'm glad you were able to make it. The Professor has been doing some fascinating work, which Tony says has an interesting tie with what you're doing. I think the PSR will give you some scientific back-up for what you are doing, as I understand it."

"And if not," Ariane said, "It will be a beautiful trip," she waved up to the azure skies all but empty of clouds. "Plus we stopped at Whole Food and have packed a delicious luncheon for all of us at Mendocino."

"Oh, I wish I had known," rued Carole, "I would have offered to bring something, too."

"But no, you are our guests," Ariane insisted. "You will have a good time today, I know."

"We already are," said Jason. "And I want to offer our congratulations on what you did in revealing the subterfuge of OPIC."

"Oh, yes," Carole echoed, "You were very courageous."

Beaming, Ariane said to Geoffrey, "We have new friends, *mon cher.*" She gave Carole a penetrating look and Jason, and then back to Carole. "You have blossomed with this man, yes?"

Carole looked at Jason and then back at Ariane. "Yes, *c'est vrai*," she said.

"*Ah, tu parles français aussi!*" Ariane said with delight.

"*Seulement un petit peu.* I'm better when I've had a glass of wine...even American wine."

They all laughed. "*Bien,*" Ariane said, "Let us get you comfortable in *Avionne* and then Geoffrey and I must sign out of the trip."

Jason noticed a slight flicker in Geoffrey's expression when she said that but said nothing. He and Carole climbed into the back seats and belted up, and Ariane and Geoffrey walked back toward the office.

"We're okay?" Geoffrey asked Ariane.

"Yes, of course. Manny went over the entire aircraft this morning. There was nothing new."

"Do you think we should tell Carole and Jason about the attempted sabotage?"

"No, *mon cher*. This was not about them." She thought for a moment. "At least not yet. It may be that later they will need to know and we can tell them."

"You're right. They don't need to worry."

They continued to the office, for show, and in a couple of minutes were back out at the plane. Geoffrey installed Ariane in the front passenger seat, checking her belt, and closing the door. Then he circled in front of the nose and got into the pilot's seat. He gave a quick safety briefing, and then started the engine. They tested the intercom system – everyone could hear each other clearly – and then he spoke with ground control. He read back his instructions and set his transponder and GPS, and then rolled out to runway 28L.

Ariane turned to Jason and Carole. "The wind is coming in from over the ocean, so we will take off to the west and fly up the coast. It is a perfect day for the flying."

"I love your accent," Carole responded.

Ariane laughed. "I think it is more pronounced when I am in *Avionne.*"

There was little traffic so Geoffrey was cleared for an immediate departure and a minute later they were climbing toward 8,500 feet. The view was spectacular, with the marine layer sitting well back from the shoreline. The myriad shades of blue and green of the Pacific were edged by the white of the surf which met the land, sometimes on beaches, often at the base of cliffs. They passed the forests that covered the coastal ridge from Santa Cruz to Pacifica, slipped through the traffic going into and coming out of SFO, and then flew by the Golden Gate. The view from the bridge itself is marvelous, but the view from above and a couple of miles to the west was stunning.

The four people in the plane were unaware that they were being tracked, though Ariane especially wouldn't have been surprised. In a computer cave with very little light except from low spots overhead and the equipment – you couldn't see faces except from the reflections off the monitors – a woman at a console was speaking to her supervisor who was standing behind her, looking at her monitor. They were watching the track of the plane up the coast. "We can take them out, sir. The plane was fitted a week ago."

"I don't think so."

"But we could do it over the ocean and it would be difficult to find any evidence," she pressed.

The supervisor looked down at the woman while she stared at the monitor. If he could have seen her face, it would have confirmed his impression from her voice that she was overly excited at the possibility of a kill.

"No, Kris, they are not a threat at this time."

"Are you sure, sir?"

"We had them checked out. They just got together. They're love birds."

"That could just be a cover..."

The supervisor took a deep breath and let it out, wondering if he was more patient with the woman than he should be. He gave it another try. "If you saw them together, you'd realize that there was little else on their minds other than each other."

"Yes, sir," the woman said, trying to hide the disappointment in her voice.

What they didn't know was that Ariane had known of the incursion into their hangar. Her no-light camera had captured the break-in and the installation of a device designed to sever the fuel line. After a crash, the cut would have never been noticed. She had had Manny Denson, a local mechanic who had worked special ops with her over the years, remove the device and trace it. She had also gotten an ID on the two men who had done the job. They were freelancers working for a San Jose alarm company that was a front, one of many, for Midas Five.

They continued north skirting the western boundaries of Marin and then Sonoma counties, and soon Geoffrey was beginning a slow descent into Little River Airport. The place was empty of traffic and people, except for an old black Crown Victoria waiting for them; a driver standing by its side. They transferred several boxes from the plane to the trunk of the car – "*C'est le dejeuner!*" Ariane told them – and piled in for the short drive back to the coast and then south to a spot several miles north of Albion, where the driver turned off onto a narrow dirt road that headed into a thick swath of eucalyptus trees. They wound through it for a half-mile, stopping once to clear a modern-looking security gate that featured a camera and a call box. Since they were expected they were cleared almost immediately and they drove on. Soon they emerged into a large meadow, surrounded by trees on three sides and fronting atop a bluff on the ocean.

"How marvelous," Carole said.

"Awesome," Jason added. "What a great spot. I could write a dozen books a year here."

As they pulled up toward the house, the front door opened and out stepped a man who could only be The Professor. He was a tall, thin man with unkempt salt-and-pepper hair but a neatly-trimmed Van Dyke beard. He was wearing a blue denim workshirt and well-worn brown corduroy slacks.

"Come in, come in," he ordered almost before they were out of the car. Geoffrey and Ariane greeted him and made the introductions to Jason and Carole. "Come in, come in," he repeated. They preceded him through the door in a large open space that was his living area.

"Oh, we brought lunch. A couple of boxes in the trunk," Geoffrey said.

"Lazlo will get it," said The Professor. He went to the door and instructed the driver to bring the boxes from the trunk and put them in the kitchen. Leaving the door open for him, The Professor led them to a door off to the side that opened onto a stairway to the basement. He went first and the four followed, with Ariane in front and Geoffrey taking up the rear.

Where the upstairs featured an eclectic mix of furniture and art from baroque to contemporary, the laboratory below was about half the size and was clean and mechanical. There were racks of electronic equipment, both computer and audio-visual. There was a pair of consoles, one the primary and one obviously the back up; it had books and other bits and pieces stacked on the table. There was a well-used chair in front of the primary terminal, and several other chairs in various spots around the room that didn't look as though they had been sat upon recently.

The Professor turned to face his four guests, and announced, "What I have developed will change the world forever."

The Professor

"What you have to understand, my dear, is that the species has been watered down in terms of its consciousness. There are simply too many people, and they have driven down the intellect of the human race. While their numbers are enormous, their intelligence is not, and so they have produced governments that fail to challenge their failed thinking, or rather lack thereof. So we over-fish the oceans, we pollute our water and air, we use chemicals to enable dead soil to produce crops.

"The unfortunate truth is we have gone past the point of being able to reduce the population incrementally. Since only 179,000 souls pass every day, it would take 88 years of no births to get the population down to a healthy level of two billion. I thought maybe we would see a nuclear exchange between India and Pakistan but that wouldn't be enough. Not only that, it would make large areas of the planet uninhabitable for decades upon decades.

"And besides, war is not a viable answer because it reduces the numbers without targeting the least useful to our survival. I'm sorry to put it in those terms, but the range of the species is quite considerable, and those who have high levels of consciousness are more valuable in the design and creation of a healthy planet. Higher consciousness is where evolution will take us – now, if we act, centuries later if we don't.

"That's why I started looking at a way to quantify and measure consciousness. Tony Seton said he explained it to you the other day. The methodology I devised looks at overall awareness which registers as hue; character as in the integration of awareness, integrity and purpose which shows as the richness of the color or lumens; and where the person's thinking is – about the past, present, or future – as demonstrated by the level chroma or brilliance of the color. If it's neon-like, the person's mind in mostly thinking about he future, if he's stuck in the past, the color is washed out. If the person is in the moment, the color is even. Using those primary criteria, you can evaluate the mind of a human being through their aura."

"The mind being the consciousness which is the heart and the brain, maybe the soul?" Jason asked.

"That is right, that is right," replied The Professor. "Yes, the soul embodies thought and character. Consciousness includes ideas and emotions, character is defined by intention and behavior." He stopped as if interrupted and looked closely at Carole and then Jason. "This does make sense, doesn't it?" He wanted to be sure.

They both nodded. They had been following him carefully, understanding what he was saying, and not wanting to fall off his track. That had managed to keep up, grateful for having been briefed by Tony two days earlier.

"Good," The Professor said, rubbing his hands together. "Now let's take a look at what consciousness, as seen through auras, actually looks like." He gestured that they should go over to the console where he had a typical computer monitor and keyboard hooked up to what looked like a standard PC. He sat himself down and Carole and Jason joined him on folding chairs which Geoffrey had placed on either side of The Professor.

"Okay," he said, tapping his keyboard, "Let me show you first what an aura looks like." He looked over at a simple home video camera sitting atop a tripod aimed at Ariane who was standing in front of a black curtain. "This is very basic. All of this equipment is off-the-shelf," he said, waving at the computer set-up. What isn't is my program which can run on the simplest of computers, and watch what it does."

The Professor tapped a series of keys and immediately there was the live head shot of Ariane standing in front of the camera. A couple of more taps and the shot widened out to provide more room about her skull. More taps, and an aura appeared around her head.

"Now you might ask why it is mostly just on top of her instead of all of her and that is because the aura is based primarily on brain activity. Yes, the heart, as we refer to it, is involved, but the integration of thoughts and emotions takes place in the cranium. You understand?"

They nodded.

"So we look at Ariane's aura and we see a being who is more conscious than most, far more conscious. And I say that not because I am fond of her" -- they watched her smile – "but because it's true. She is. I think you know that." More nodding. "Her aura is a bright dark blue, you call it indigo, and the color is solid; there is no translucency. Also, it is easy to see and to look at. I know that doesn't sound scientific, but when you've seen colors that are fading or some that are almost too bright to look at, then you know what you don't want. So these three factors show that she has a high degree of awareness, she has character, and she is engaged. That is why I say that she is very conscious."

"Tony told us about the corona," Jason ventured.

"Ah yes, well as you can see here, the top of her aura is very smooth. The corona, ha, ha, yes. It also shows commitment. Sometimes when it is erratic – Tony used the word sparking, I think that is good – it is a sign of disturbance. I added this factor because someone can be consistent but can also be mad, or evil."

"Consistently so," Carole offered.

"That's right," The Professor said. "Now I presume you wouldn't want to pass up the opportunity to see your own auras, am I correct?"

Carole and Jason looked at each other. "Yes, please," she said. "Jason saw mine but I never saw his. And can we see our own?"

"Certainly," said The Professor. "I save them all."

Jason walked over to where Ariane was standing and took her place. He looked at the camera. Ariane walked back to where Geoffrey stood behind Carole watching the demonstration. "Oh gracious," Carole said toward Jason with false alarm, and then she giggled. "Just kidding."

Everyone laughed with her, except The Professor, who remonstrated her, "This is not a parlor trick, you know."

"Sorry," said a clearly chastened Carole.

The image on the screen was not dissimilar from Ariane's. Maybe it wasn't quite as blue, but it was certainly as solid. The chroma was a little higher and his corona was almost imperceptibly less smooth. The Professor said it was likely so because this was his first experience with PSR and he might be a bit nervous. Even as they stared at the screen, the chroma seemed to lower slightly and the corona to smooth out.

"Did he do that deliberately?" Carole asked. "Can someone change their aura if they want?"

"Very important question," The Professor said, ameliorating his earlier comment to her. "Yes and no. Yes, he did it by feeling more comfortable. He knew that he was good and that reduced his nervousness. But can an evil or crazy person change their appearance by adjusting their thoughts and feelings, I can say categorically no, they can't. And the reason is that they can't fool all four indices. That's why I designed it this way. That is why this system is so critical, and foolproof."

"My turn," Carole said and she walked over to Jason, resisting the desire to tease him or even touch him, but she gave him a loving smile. She centered herself toward the camera as Jason regained his seat.

"Oh ho," said The Professor, "I don't see this often. You two are almost identical. Like Geoffrey and Ariane." He tapped some keys and he told Carole to come back and take her seat. Then he put her aura up on the screen first, giving her a chance to examine it, and then showing a comparison shot with Jason's aura. "You see, very little difference. And this is not a function of partnering per se. Many people get together with very different auras and they live very good lives, but I don't know of any couples with similar auras who don't get along well because they are in the same evolutionary place of consciousness."

The Professor stood up and faced them all. "I have some work to do upstairs with Ariane, but Geoffrey will give you a further demonstration of PSR. We can talk further later." And with that he and Ariane left them. (They didn't know at the time that she was make final arrangements with him for the release of a consumer version of the software.)

"That was very neat," said Jason, curbing his enthusiasm. "So we could be the new kinds of Doublemint twins," he joked. They all laughed.

Geoffrey took The Professor's seat and set up the computer to apply the PSR software to other sources, specifically files on the computer and images from the Internet. He provided Carole and Jason with a series of pictures of people from the headlines with their auras clearly displayed. There were very few surprises, but there were a few. Geoffrey displayed a shot of Bobby Kennedy during the early Sixties when he was Attorney General and then another when he was running for president in 1968, a week before he was assassinated.

"It's quite amazing the difference," Geoffrey pointed out. "The level of his consciousness rose dramatically between those two shots. Such a difference, as we checked out on other people, requires some sort of epiphany."

"Come to Jesus? Born-again?"

"It funny you should mention that, Jason, because it has nothing to do with religion. In fact everyone we looked at who was known for their religiosity was in the yellow-green region. They were not very conscious. They might be solid colors and their chroma level and corona could be even, but it would suggest that while they were moral and purposeful, they weren't seeing the larger picture. Of course there are exceptions, like the Dalai Lama and those who hold to the true Christ Consciousness."

"So it wasn't that they were bad or anything, but that they were limited in their thinking, is that right?" Carole asked.

"Exactly. They were stuck in their belief system and couldn't see beyond it. Wouldn't look beyond it," Geoffrey replied.

He created a split screen with four separate regions. In one he put a shot of fans at an Alabama football game, in a second he put graduate students in a Harvard philosophy lecture hall, in a third he put a floor scene at the New York Stock Exchange, and the fourth was of babies in a maternity ward. "The Professor tweaked the software so that it could display the consciousness not just of individuals but of groups of people; averaging out all of the people in the shot." He tapped a key, and all of the groups were displayed with a collective aura.

"Holy moly," Jason said.

"I love it," Carole said. "The babies have the best color although it's a little pale. I would guess that's because they haven't developed their own minds in the world."

"That's what we thought," Geoffrey confirmed.

"And the students show a higher consciousness and have their colors filled in, but there's a wide range in the chroma," she observed. "I supposed that's to be expected for people of that age."

"And the pressure of Harvard, methinks," Jason added. "The Wall Streeters seem to be not very conscious but very determined. Am I reading that right, Geoffrey?"

"That's the way we interpreted it."

"And the football fans? Low everything it looks like," Jason observed.

Geoffrey turned away from the computer to face him. "The Professor thinks this represents a mob mentality, in that they subsume themselves to a cause. They don't think for themselves. We found the same levels in church as we did at sporting events."

"That makes sense, doesn't it?" Carole said. "Consciousness is about being conscious, after all. People thinking on their own to reach a higher consciousness. Not following someone else's lead."

Geoffrey cleared the screen and brought up a split screen. On one side was a series of photos of the most impoverished people of the world, from India, South America, and Africa, as well as from some Northern Hemisphere ghettos. On the other side were people who were doing well, financially. There were scenes from symphony audiences, high-end restaurants, black-tie parties, and other upscale events.

"I don't think it comes as a surprise that the poor on our planet have a low level of consciousness, thin colors, and low chroma. Their view of the world and life is minimalist. They are mostly focused on basic survival. Morality falls behind simply staying alive. And they lack hope. On the other side, there is greater awareness, but again the color is somewhat thin which we might interpret as their separation from much of the world."

"That's how they got to where they are," observed Carole.

"That's right. Their chroma range isn't large, which indicates that they are probably unruffled by their lives, for the most part."

Jason took a deep breath and let it out slowly and somewhat noisily between his teeth.

"I think Jason has a thought," Carole said.

"I was thinking that this confirms what we've thought all along," he said.

"And?" she asked.

"It will make it easier for the more conscious people, in our society especially, to comprehend ."

After a few more minutes of looking at various people with their auras, Jason said he thought they'd seen enough. Carole agreed, and they went upstairs to join The Professor and Ariane. She had brought out the boxes of prepared food that they had taken with them on the plane, and while the three had been downstairs, she had laid out a marvelous buffet for everyone. There was salmon and smoked trout, pulled pork, tri-tip and various cheeses; a half-dozen different salads, breads and rolls, and condiments; soft drinks, fruit drinks, and a bottle of red wine and a bottle of white. Geoffrey rued that he couldn't enjoy the Heller Estate Cabernet because he was flying, calling it one of the best organic reds he'd tasted in a long time.

"This is why we are friends," The Professor said. It was his most serious attempt at humor all morning, and a sign that he was lightening up. Tony had warned them that he was leery about visitors in general, even if they were clearly allies.

They all filled their plates, took their drinks and sat on chairs and couches around a large coffee table in the middle of the living room. Of course the conversation was about auras and PSR.

The Professor explained that a major reason that most people in the developed nations don't realize what they're missing in auras was purely a business matter. "It was because of greed, you know. We don't see auras because the person behind the most successful television picture tube at the time of its development wanted to sell his process which used RBG guns to make all colors, instead of RYB which worked with a much more simplified and less expensive system."

Geoffrey explained, "RBG is red, blue, and green. Those three color guns make up all of the images you see on a video monitor. Using RYB – red, yellow, and blue guns – was a much better system which produced colors that accustomed human retinas to seeing auras."

Ariane added, "It was the brilliance of The Professor that he created his algorithms to make it easier to for the human eye to adjust from red-green-blue to the red-yellow-blue image, and so as to see the auras."

"Capitalism strikes again, eh?" Jason asked.

"You can call it that, of course. It was just the power of the wallet. The company that owned the patent on the RGB design paid off federal regulators – and the politicians who oversaw them – to make sure that the RBG system was approved."

"That's like the Dvorak keyboard being eclipsed by the Qwerty model," Carole offered, "even though you can type much faster on the Dvorak because the most commonly used keys are under the stronger fingers."

"Yes, young lady, that's exactly right."

Carole blushed.

The professor continued, "Geoffrey, tell them about the movie film analogy you are using."

"After seeing auras visibly, your system understands and reads them without seeing the colors. Your third eye perceives the aura subliminally. And yes, as The Professor said, we're using this image in his explainer. It's like in the old days when a projector wasn't working right and showed a movie at fewer than twenty-eight frames a second. You'd see the spaces between the frames and the frame lines. Right?"

"Yes," Jason said. "Especially when my father ran the eight millimeter home movies."

"That's it," Geoffrey said. "Similarly, when you increase your level of consciousness, you see the same information as is in the aura without noticing the colors. If that makes sense."

It did. They ate in silence for a moment, and then Carole asked, "Professor, when word gets out about auras, what do you think is going to happen?"

The Professor took another bite of the smoked trout on his plate, and after chewing and swallowing it, he sent it down with a sip of the Heller Cab. "I'm glad you're doing the flying, Geoffrey. It means more of this wine for me. Thank you." There was amusement all around. "The simple answer is that I don't know. Of course, how could I, but in all honesty I must say that while I'm optimistic about the long term, I think the immediate future will be full of rancor and violence. I once thought that I should be bothered by what this invention would induce. I might have thought myself to be the greatest mass murderer in the history of the world." He took a taste of some German potato salad, and then punctuating his thoughts with his fork he said, "But I don't see it that way. All PSR does is restore a natural human ability that was taken from us by primitive thinking, and then mostly buried in this past century by corporate avarice. But I also know that there are millions of people around the world who are very conscious people who would love to live in a society that is built around peace instead of war, and filling needs instead of wants manufactured by the advertising industry. PSR will make that possible."

"Will we see it in our lifetimes?" Jason asked.

"Whose lifetime?" The Professor asked and laughed. "I'm not trying to evade the lady's question. It could be quite bleak for a while. First, when the concept of consciousness suddenly becomes ubiquitous, there will be an upwelling of anger by those who are toward the bottom of the consciousness ladder. They will feel under attack; most of them are paranoid to begin with, so they will strike out. But there will also be people who will have been holding themselves back because of the circumstances of their lives, and they will climb out from under the proverbial rock which has been shielding them. They will put themselves in more hospitable environments and will succeed, often dramatically, in expanding their awareness. This will be a wonderful thing, mostly.

"Still, I expect that there will be considerable chaos, with governments stymied and unable to do very much. I wouldn't be surprised if we didn't see a vast move of like-minded people to form their own communities."

"Like the communes of the Sixties and Seventies," Geoffrey put in. "Except better organized and more purposeful. Not hiding places but growing places."

The Professor cleared his throat and took back the floor. "One of the surprises, perhaps, will be the withdrawal of support for the vast numbers of people who have relied on that support from people on the outside. Especially in the southern hemisphere. More conscious does not mean more liberal. The more conscious people will realize that perpetuating the lives of billions of people who are at risk, already living on the edge, is destructive for the future of the Earth. I would expect that they would somehow provide a lifeline for the most conscious people in those zones. Those who can escape will escape, I think."

A pall took over the room. Other than the sounds of eating and drinking, and the ocean not far away, there was silence. It was The Professor who broke it. "Our dear blue planet can sustain a population of about two billion people. We have seven billion. We have done great damage to the ecosystem already. If we don't act quickly to reduce the demand on resources – by reducing the number of people seeking them – then it will push the environment past a point where it might recover but for centuries. That would be less responsible than recognizing the truth, and acting for the survival of the species. Is it a Hobson's choice? Some will see it that way. I don't. I am excited at what the world will be like when we restore the natural balances. Not to sound retributive, but we got ourselves into this disaster through our blind ignorance, our denial, our foolishness, our corruption, our degenerate false morals perpetuated by religion. It's time to do it right. Yes, it will have to start in even my lifetime, though how long it will take to find our natural balance, I don't know. I hope you all will see it."

The Hero Dawg

The flight back to Monterey was awesome, partly because of the stunning view of the Central California Coast from 7,500 feet but they had seen that before. There was also the huge responsibility generated by their conversations with The Professor that weighed on them. Geoffrey and Ariane had been familiar with the ramifications of unleashing PSR on the unsuspecting world. As Geoffrey had noted to them as he was pre-flighting the airplane at the Little River airstrip, it really wasn't a choice. The car was headed over the cliff; was it wrong for some people to jump out? To which Jason had replied, "We can call it *Rebel with a Cause.*" Only Ariane hadn't seen the James Dean film and it was quickly explained to her. At the end of the flight, they disembarked with expressions that seemed to indicate that the beauty of the ocean meeting the shore had perhaps somewhat mitigated the enormity of the work that was before them.

After thanking Geoffrey and Ariane for the flight and the lunch and the time with The Professor, Jason and Carole drove home. The sight of a black sedan at the curb near their driveway did not auger well. Jason pulled into the driveway and they were disturbed to see a man sitting on the front porch but then relieved to see that The Dawg was standing next to him receiving rubbies. Of course The Dawg had heard them coming several blocks away, recognizing the unique sound of the motor, so he was wagging his tail and waiting for them to get out of the car. As they did so, the man stood up and began walking slowly toward them.

"Mr. Isaac, right?"

"Right," Jason said, his voice resonant with concern, or at least questions. It was amazing how powerful was The Dawg's influence on him.

"I'm Mike Olsen with the FBI." He displayed his credentials to Jason and nodded his head to Carole.

"What's this all about?" Carole asked, a slight sharpness in her tone. Jason later told her how much he liked that, that he had found in her an ally he'd never known before.

"You are Miz Holley, I'm thinking," he said amiably.

"You'd be thinking right," she told him, "But now I'd also like to know how you knew that."

Yes, ma'am," he said, shifting his attention from Jason to Carole. "There was an break-in here at the house."

"What?" they both said at the same time.

Olsen put up both his hands and said, "Not to worry. They didn't take anything. They were just on an exploratory mission. And the police got here maybe two minutes after they made their entry." He looked down at The Dawg who was now standing between Jason and Carole looking at the agent, as they were. "Your dog saved the day. He called the cops. He's apparently part of some canine crime prevention program?"

"That's right," said Jason, relief creeping into his voice. "I'll explain it later," he told Carole, "when we are feeding him some steak for dinner tonight." The Dawg's tail wagged harder.

"I think he understood you," the agent said puzzled.

"Of course he did, Mr. Olsen, or do I call you Agent Olsen," Carole said to him.

"Call me, Mike, please."

"All right, Mike, he's very bright," Carole said, "Brighter than most people, we think."

"So what were these people doing?" Jason wanted to know. "How did they get in? Are they in jail? Who are they?"

Carole touched Jason's arm. "Perhaps we might invite him to come into the house."

"Good idea," Jason said. "Pardon my manners, um, Mike. Please come in."

They went inside and Jason walked all around the downstairs looking carefully here and there. "Did they get upstairs?" he asked from the bottom of the staircase.

"No," the agent said, "As I said, the Monterey police were here probably two minutes after they got in. I don't know how they got in. We didn't see any signs of forced entry."

"We leave the door open," Carole told him. "This is - was? - a safe neighborhood. We only lock the doors at night before we go to bed."

"That would explain the entry," he acknowledged, with just a tinge of remonstrance for the casual security plan they employed. "Judging from the equipment they carried, they weren't intent on stealing anything, just looking at what was here. They had a pair of listening devices, bugs, that they were probably going to plant here, but mostly they were looking. They were wearing rubber gloves that are designed for such a search."

"Such a search," Jason echoed. "And you're FBI. There's more to this than meets the eye, so to say."

"Yessir, there is. The two men were employees of a private security agency, an offshoot of what used to be called Blackwater. The cops got that from the information in their wallets, including business cards. You wouldn't think those people would be carrying identification, but I guess they didn't think they'd be caught. They probably knew that you would be away from the house for some time."

Carole and Jason looked at each other. "We were up in Mendocino. I wonder how they knew that."

"Well as I said, they seemed to know what they were doing, except for your dog."

"And where are they now?"

"They are in custody. The Monterey police turned them over to us because they said they were connected to the Department of Homeland Security."

Jason's fuse burned down in a flash. "What? What are those yahoos doing looking in our house? We're not terrorists. Are they allowed to do that?"

Agent Olsen shook he head patiently. "No, of course not. Not unless they have a warrant, and they didn't. Unfortunately, the Patriot Act allows to them to get a warrant without probably cause, but as I said, they didn't have a warrant, and we're pretty sure that it was a made up story. But because they invoked a federal agency, they were handed over to the Bureau. We've brought them up to our San Francisco office until we can get this all sorted out."

Jason calmed himself down. "This world has gone nuts," he said, mostly to Carole.

"May I get you something to drink or eat, Mike?" Carole asked him.

"Oh, no thank you, Miz Holley, I'll be going in just a minute. I just wanted to be here with you when you got home, to assure you that nothing had been taken, and to find out if you knew why these men were in your house."

Carole looked at Jason.

"Oh, and I got your name off the luggage tag on the bag on the back deck, and I checked the registration on the car out front."

"Ah," Carole said.

The agent waited and when nothing was volunteered, he asked again, "So would you know why these men had come into your house? What they might have been looking for?"

"You mean drugs or contraband of some sort?" Jason asked.

"That's not what they seemed to be looking for."

"What do you think they were looking for?" Carole asked him.

"We don't know. There are no files on either of you. You're not suspected of anything or associated with any criminal elements." Olsen gave a short laugh. "The only thing we could guess was that they were trying to discover the plot of your latest book."

Carole looked sharply at Jason but he kept his eyes on the FBI agent. "That would make about as much sense as anything I could imagine," he said.

"Maybe they had the wrong house," Carole ventured.

The agent looked at her for a moment, clearly wondering if she was trying to divert his attention from them. Whatever he thought wasn't obvious. "It's possible, but these guys were pros. Not likely to make such a mistake."

"Why do I not find that comforting?" Jason asked rhetorically.

"You'd know better than I, apparently," Olsen said evenly.

"All right," Jason said, "I'm not going to get in your way on this. The only thing I can think of is that we went up north to Mendocino to meet with a professor who is involved in some interesting experiments about consciousness. But this is just a man, maybe a little eccentric," he said, turning to Carole who nodded her agreement, "working alone in the basement of his home. He isn't any kind of spy, for goodness sakes."

"He's more like a recluse, from what I could see," Carole told him, shaking her head.

"Mike, did you by any chance check our house for bugs?"

The agent looked at Jason for a long moment. "Actually we did. We wanted to make sure that the two bugs they had in their pockets were the only ones they brought with them." He knew from their expressions that they didn't know if they could trust him and he responded to that. "I know you don't know if you can believe me, but I have a suggestion for you."

"What's that?" Jason asked.

"You have a smartphone, don't you?"

Carole answered, "Yes, we both do."

Olsen took a business card out of his wallet and a pen and wrote on the back of the card. When he was done he handed it to her. "That's an app you can download onto your phone and it detects listening devices up to a hundred feet away."

"Bug Buster. How clever," Carole read from the card. "Thank you. I'm sorry if I seemed rude to you. I've never encountered anything like this before." She looked to Jason. "This isn't our country any more, Jason."

"No, no it isn't," he agreed with her in a distracted voice.

The FBI man stood up. "I'm sorry you feel that way, but off the record, I agree with you. Since 911, maybe before, it's not the country I was brought up to think it was. But I can tell you, there are some of us in law enforcement who are as unhappy with what's going on as you are, and we're doing our best to distinguish us in the white hats from those who wear something else. If that helps," he added.

"I think it does," Carole said. "And thank you."

Jason walked him to the door, where he thanked him, and watched him walk down the driveway and turn to the street. Then he closed the door and returned to Carole, taking her in his arms. "What have we gotten ourselves into?" she asked, concern clarion in her voice.

"I don't know," Jason said, "But I'm glad we're in it together. Not that I ever thought it would be like this, or that I would have put you in any danger. You know what I mean?"

"Yes, dearest Jason, I do, and I feel the same way."

They held each other closely for a long minute and then were interrupted in their silence by a sort of whimpering sound by The Dawg.

They laughed. "You were the hero, Dawg, and you want that steak I promised you, is that it?"

The Dawg wagged his tail.

"And you, my dear," Jason said to Carole, "a glass of wine maybe, and something to nibble on?"

"I'll get the nibbles, you get the wine."

The Dawg whimpered.

"After you get him his steak."

"Woof," said The Dawg.

"And will you explain to me what he did to earn a steak?"

Jason chuckled, "Come with me, my pretty," he said as he took her hand and led her through the kitchen to the back door. "Back in just a moment, pal. Just want to show her the scene of your triumph."

The Dawg woofed again.

Jason opened the door and brought Carole out onto the back deck. In a corner, hidden from obvious view by a tool shed, there was a loose shingle on the side of the house. Jason knelt down. Carole bent over. Jason carefully slid the shingle, which was held by a single nail at the top center so that it turned clockwise, uncovering a red button the size of a half-dollar.

"What's that?" Carole asked.

"It's a 911 emergency connect button. The Dawg has been taught to move the shingle out of the way and push that button if there is ever any danger at the house. It rings directly through to the central dispatch."

"You're serious, aren't you? Oh my goodness. I've never seen anything like that." Carole laughed. "How bizarre."

"The Dawg is one of a dozen dogs on the Peninsula who are part of a test program."

"And what does he do then, make three short barks, then three long barks, then three short barks to send an SOS?"

Jason laughed. "You think that's funny. The police wanted to figure out a way to make sure that there were no false alarms."

"You mean like The Dawg would press the button thinking

someone would bring over his dinner?" Carole burst out laughing.

"They didn't know."

"And...?"

"And so far at least, and the program has been running two years," Jason told her, pride rising in his voice, "they haven't needed anything else. And, Miss Hoity Toity, there hasn't been a single false alarm."

"Ah, and has anyone been saved from dastardly deed doers?" Carole asked, her eyebrows at peak extension.

"They have foiled three burglaries that I'm aware of, and brought firefighters to a home when a hot plate shorted out and started a small fire. They put it out before it did any serious damage."

"And now The Dawg has caught a couple of spies," Carole said. She took his hand and led him back to the door, "Come on Sherlock, The Dawg certainly does deserve a steak."

While Jason was preparing the steak for The Dawg, Carole felt a need to roam the house. She spent several minutes upstairs and then several more down, looking behind things and underneath others. She returned to the kitchen where Jason was cooking the steak. "He likes it medium rare," he explained. "Should be ready in a couple of minutes," he said cheerfully.

"I wouldn't want to miss it," Carole told them both. "Jason?"

"Yes, Carole?"

"What do you think of the idea of my downloading that BugBuster app and checking the house? You wouldn't think I'm overly paranoid, would you?"

"Not at all, my dear. We don't know what were dealing with

here. That doesn't seem paranoid to me. Go for it."

"Thanks," she told him with an appreciative smile.

"Thank you," he said.

Carole pulled her phone out of the pocket of her coat which was hanging on the back of a chair. While Jason finished up cooking the steak, she found and downloaded the app. With the steak cooling on a plate, Carole ran the app. She went back upstairs and was down in less than a minute. "I think Mike of the FBI was right. They did get them in time. This says there's nothing operating in or near the house. If it knows what it is doing, of course."

"Of course," said Jason. He carved up the steak into bite-sized pieces.

"Are you going to feed him each piece?" Carole asked him.

"Would that be over the top?" he returned.

"Probably, but he is a hero, so I'd be reluctant to make a federal case out of it."

"Federal case," Jason repeated, "That was very good."

"Even though it wasn't deliberate?" she asked, her eyebrows raised.

"Maybe especially so. I know what I'll do." He went over to The Dawg's food dish in a corner of the kitchen. He scraped a third of the steak into the dish. "I'll dole it out to him. It will make the pleasure last longer."

"Jason?"

"Yes, Carole."

"I was feeling icky because of those men here. I think I'll take a shower, if that's all right."

"I understand fully, my dearest," Jason told her. "Good idea.

Wash those men right outta your hair."

"With apologies to Mary Martin." She gave him a big smile and trotted up the stairs.

Jason watched The Dawg enjoying his special dinner. "Don't gorge yourself, pal," he said. "I'll give you the rest of this later. Okay?" The Dawg didn't respond. He was too busy enjoying his steak.

Jason put the plate down on the prep-island and then looked upstairs as he heard the water running. "Later, Dawg," he said and quietly climbed the stairs. Carole was in the shower. Jason slid over to the stereo table and quickly found the CD he was looking for; hey, he had them all in alphabetical order. He turned on the player and amplifier and pushed in the disc. Then he forwarded it to a special selection. Soon the strains of Robert Preston from *The Music Man* filled the room, and no doubt reached Carole in the bathroom.

Jason peeked through the half-open door and saw a wide smile of pleasure on Carole's face. Yes, she could hear the music. He took off his clothes and went over to the stereo and turned it down. Then he walked into the bathroom singing.

> *There was love all around*
> *But I never heard it singing*
> *No I never heard it at all*
> *Till there was you*

He made sure by the change in her expression that she knew it was he and not Preston. Her eyes were closed because she was in the process of washing her hair and she didn't want soap in them. He opened the door to the shower and got in with her, putting his arms around her, and still singing.

Her eyes still closed, she put her arms around him and they sang together,

Till there was you.

He kissed her on her neck and face, wherever he could find a spot without soap on it. Then he explained, "I thought you might need help scrubbing your back."

"Why would that be?" she asked coyly.

"Because you might have your own arms wrapped around my back."

"You are such a smart man. No wonder I love you."

A Word with the Wise

"Jason, darling," Carole said the next morning as they lay atop the sheets, sleep long gone from their eyes, but an expression of charmed languor on their faces.

"Carole, darling," Jason responded.

"I was thinking," she started.

"Not recently, I hope. You seemed fully in the moment. Normal chroma and all that."

Carole laughed. "My chroma was fine, thank you. It was afterwards, like here entwined with you. That's when."

"Not to interrupt, but were you aware that you have two bedroom voices," Jason told her. "One is before we make love. It's husky, it's deep, it's primal, it's Aphrodite. The other is after when your brain takes off from a plateau of feeling nourished when you are in the Psyche mode and your mind is wrapped around tomorrow, and how to make it better."

"That sounds all right, to me, I think," Carole replied. "Does it work for you?"

"Uh, ya know, I have a little bit of a problem with that."

"Oh, and how, pray tell, could you possibly have a problem with that?"

Jason rolled her off of him onto her back and rolled himself on top of her. Carole put her arms around him. In a soft but deep voice he said to her, "The problem with that is that when you get into that brilliant Psyche voice, it turns me on."

"Yes, go on," Carole said, her voice down an octave.

"I don't want you to think that I am not interested in or am ignoring your mind, you know."

"I don't think it's something you have to worry about," she said, pulling his face closer to hers. "You know why?"

"Why?"

"Because I know you think I'm brilliant."

"Oh, phew."

"And because there's always time to think."

With that, what she had been thinking about was postponed for a later discussion.

That later discussion occurred when hunger drove them downstairs to the breakfast table. Carole thought they should check in with the beings upstairs and find out if they had anything to add to what they had learned in Mendocino. Jason added that they might also ask about the spies in their house. But first they had a delicious breakfast, at which The Dawg got the last of his streak; reheated, of course. Then they adjourned to the office and Jason called out for Klaatu. In seconds their three heavenly contacts appeared on the screen.

"Hello, y'all... Carole thought it would be a good idea to check in with you after our meeting with The Professor. What a remarkable fellow. He seems to have the scientific piece and we have the social piece. Is that right?"

136

"Oh excellent Jason, and Carole," Klaatu said gleaming. He looked at his two colleagues and they were both clearly pleased as well. "Quite so indeed."

"We were wondering if there was anything else we needed to understand about where we were headed before we got started."

Sinead spoke. "I think they would benefit from knowing how we got to where we are. Don't you agree, SueLan?"

"Most emphatically," came her reply. They both looked to Klaatu, who nodded his agreement to them.

"The problem," explained Klaatu, "is that when the First and Second World had reached something of a plateau, where most everyone had what they needed, they forgot to advance. Smooth evolution requires volition. The whole purpose of the human race was to move itself forward, symbiotically, both as a species and individually. But people neglected themselves. They ate too much, watched hundreds of hours of television every month, played video games. They watched sports instead of getting exercise. They ate junk food instead of regarding their bodies as a temple. They stopped reading or otherwise stimulating their minds. It was like plants stopping with photosynthesis. And so their minds began to atrophy, and their failure to move themselves forward meant that their capacity to cope with the changing environment slipped ever further behind."

With a note of impatience, Sinead jumped in. "You know what it was like? People failed to upgrade their computer platform. They stayed at Windows 3.1 instead of upgrading to 7. This meant that the new, evolved programs, designed to work on a higher platform, wouldn't function."

Klaatu looked at her with interest. She looked back at him and then back at the camera. Klaatu said, "Does that make sense to you, Jason and Carole?"

"Uh-huh," Jason said. "Conceptually, but what does that mean in terms of what you wanted me to do?"

Carole said quietly, "I think he's explaining that what you're about isn't for everyone."

On the screen, Klaatu nodded sagely. "Quite that, yes."

SueLan interjected, "We don't want you to think this sloth-fulness was our idea, really. We never sanctioned, let alone encouraged, laziness."

"No, no, no," said Klaatu. "We tried to encourage people to take responsibility. That's why we installed so many of those elephant people in your government."

"He means Republicans," Sinead inserted.

"Oh yes, quite right," Klaatu said with an appreciative smile in her direction. "They were supposed to be conservatives, you know, the way they were always trumpeting" – he tittered at his pun – "about personal responsibility."

"And not getting involved in foreign wars, and balancing the budget," added Sinead with considerable disgust in her voice.

"Don't forget conservation," said SueLan, clearly disappointed.

"They said they wanted the downtrodden to start being responsible, but they took away all of the tools that might have helped them. Decent housing, better health care, good schools," Klaatu told them, "All the while insisting that it was their fault that they were falling further behind because they weren't praying hard enough."

"And that they were being subverted by homosexuals and abortionists," Sinead said.

"I don't think they'd like you folks on Fox," Jason said, "but of course you're right."

"So, um, why did you let that happen?" Carole asked gently.

There was a long silence at the other end. "Is it okay if I ask that?" She asked. "I mean, excuse me, I wasn't in on this originally."

Jason gave her a peck on the cheek. "You're as much a part of this as I am, Carole. They fixed us up, after all."

"After all they did, didn't they?" she confirmed brightly, confidence flowing in her new voice.

Klaatu cleared his throat. "That's certainly a fair question, Miss Holley, and of course you are integral in this plot."

Carole looked pleased.

"And in answer to your question, it's rather complicated."

"No it isn't, Klaatu," Sinead interrupted him.

"Oh, you think not?" It was a genuine question.

"No. We picked these people because they were ahead of the rest, most of the rest. They can understand better than most of the people you've thought about recruiting."

"I suppose that's true," Klaatu admitted, "Perhaps you'd explain then?

Sinead nodded and launched into an explanation. "There is a dialectic between Heaven and Earth. People are supposed to intrinsically find purpose in progress. They are supposed to learn from their mistakes. They are supposed to value creativity. They are supposed to love good." She snorted, "But over the millennia, various snake oil salesmen claimed that they were supposed to love god, and it all went downhill from there. People found it easier to say that they believed in god instead of good, and when things didn't go right, they could say that they had insulted their god. Religion became a fig leaf for personal failure."

"It was god's will," SueLan intoned, almost mockingly. "Only it was a false image of god. A much smaller idea of the power of the universe. Made in their own image, they said, so you can imagine just how limited their gods were.

"Yeah," said Sinead, "It was their idea of letting themselves off the hook when their plans didn't work out or someone screwed up big time."

"So for the last several thousand of your years, our work got off track," Klaatu added. "We lost control of the experiment."

"Experiment?" Carole and Jason echoed at the same time. "This sounds like a Douglas Adams sci-fi story, where the universe is being run by white lab mice," Jason added.

"Oh no," SueLan responded. "We're not lab mice. No indeed. We are people from the Atlantis era. They gave us this assignment to see if we could get the human race back on track...so to speak."

"So to speak," Klaatu said.

"And the Republicans were just a big mistake?" Jason asked.

Sinead's old petulance seemed ready to surface again. "I don't know that you have to put it that way."

Carole mediated. "I don't think he means that was the sum total of your work. You did very well in a lot of areas, especially the arts and technology. But you didn't give the creative people the authority they needed to control the greed. Is that right?"

"Quite so, Miss Holley," Klaatu said, showing his fondness for Carole. "The liberals seemed unwilling to get their hands dirty in the management of the species."

"The creative people," put in SueLan, "wanted everyone to do what they were capable of doing so they could just be creative. But some of the people who weren't interested in actually making an effort slipped into shameful indolence and their desire to have it – what was the word, Sinead, cushy?" – Sinead nodded – "made them willing to follow the demagogues who told them they could have it cushy so long as they followed their leader."

"It's like government failing to rein in capitalism," Jason noted. "But for goodness sakes, that's kind of a big slip up on your part, isn't it? It's like giving the big guns to the bad guys."

There was more silence from the screen. Then Klaatu explained, "It seems we had the same sort of issues up here which made it difficult to make things better down there "

Jason and Carole were silent. Then Carole asked, "So you brought Jason up there to start something down here?"

"Something like that, yes," Klaatu acknowledged.

"What are your expectations?" she asked. "If you have any?" Her tone wasn't rude, in fact it was tinged with compassionate understanding.

Klaatu was thoughtful. SueLan wore a pained expression. Sinead spoke. "Actually we don't," she admitted. "We're sort of shooting craps."

"Oh, Sinead," SueLan scolded, "It's not like that at all."

"Oh really, Miss Goody Two Shoes, and how would you describe it?"

"Sinead, I don't think you have to take that attitude," SueLan retorted. "We're planning to trim down the Earth's population from seven billion to two. I hardly think that's Miss Goody Two Shoes, do you?"

Sinead chuckled, "I doubt the five billion would think so."

"Excuse me," Carole said, "But you're not putting this, uh,

trimming on our shoulders?"

"Oh no," Klaatu said reassuringly, at least to himself. "Quite the opposite. You are going to save two billion people."

"Why does this sound like the glass is half full instead of half empty?" Jason asked cautiously.

"I think you discussed this with The Professor yesterday," Klaatu told him. "As far as our role in the over-population, we thought at some point that you would wake up and realize that you were committing bloaticide. Only animals with damaged brains would eat themselves to death. We were confused. There were so many wonderful people, and yet we saw you killing yourselves."

"The only one who made sense," Sinead added caustically, "was George Carlin who took the environmentalists to task. The Earth will always be around, he said, and he was right. So what if you all kill yourselves and poison the Earth, the Earth will recover. It's not in a hurry."

"We did try, you know," SueLan sounded like she was on the verge of tears. "We sent all sorts of fine people down there to try to turn things around. Just in the last century. Theodore Roosevelt, Eleanor Roosevelt, Pablo Picasso, John and Robert Kennedy, Martin Luther King, John Lennon. Of course, you killed some of them before they could have any real effect."

"Not to pick a nit," Jason came back quietly, "but I kinda resent being held responsible for their deaths."

"Oh, oh, no, I didn't mean you."

"She was referring to the species," Klaatu said, realizing that the explanation wasn't really needed.

"He was being polemical," Carole explained.

"Yes, of course," Klaatu said, his voice trailing off.

"So where does that leave us?" she asked. She had her eyes on the screen but she felt Jason's gaze on her. She looked over at him quickly and gave him a smile before turning back for her answer.

"Where we are is that we need you two to put out a message that those who are ready to move forward can see," he said.

"And take to heart," SueLan added. "Figuratively. They have to use their minds this time. Their thoughts, not just their emotions."

"And you think that these two billion better people will suddenly be able to see auras, and that will fix things?" Jason asked skeptically.

"No and yes," came the answer from the screen.

Sinead wanted to get this conversation done. "The no is that it won't be sudden. We're thinking three to five years. The yes is that there will be incredible turmoil as people become aware of the power and are forced back on themselves to obtain the proper results." She paused, and then continued. "We think it could get a bit ugly as those people who aren't ready will stage a revolt..."

"Yes, but eventually," SueLan put in, trying to rosy up the glasses, "it will all work itself out."

"You're saying that it won't be pretty reducing by five billion people?" Jason said.

"How could it not be?" asked Sinead. "But if it eases your conscience, if that's what is bothering you, it will be people who aren't conscious, who haven't answered to themselves. Violent felons, drug abusers, alcoholics, and obese people."

"Plus the corrupt politicians and the greed-besotted corporatists," put in SueLan.

"There really isn't any choice," Klaatu said, "Other than to clean the slate entirely and start over from the amoeba."

"It doesn't sound so ugly then, does it, darling?" Carole asked brightly.

"Huh," answered Jason noncommittally.

"That sums it up, I think," Carole agreed. "Oh," she caught herself, "what about those spies or whoever they were here in our house?"

"Mmm," said Klaatu, "yes, that must have been disconcerting."

Sinead picked up the explanation, "But your animal was there to call the police so everything worked out."

Carole and Jason looked at each other, then he asked, "Are you saying The Dawg is one of your agents?"

SueLan giggled, "He's not an agent. He's a gift."

"Ahso," Jason said, as if that were an answer. "So what about those two men?"

"They are from the dark side," Sinead told them. "as they say in your *Star Wars* movie. They are working with Midas Five. They thought you might have information about The Professor."

"And...?" Carole asked.

"Not to worry," she was told. "They won't bother you again."

"Why do I not feel sure about that?" Jason asked.

Klaatu told him, "We have them being held in San Francisco for the next week. Then they will be sent back to the Virginia some place for retraining. We made it look as though they mishandled the assignment."

"Oh, good," Carole responded. "And they won't send anyone else to investigate us."

"No, my dear," Klaatu said assuringly. "We gave them to believe that you weren't a threat to them. That you were a couple of romantics who needn't be bothered about."

Carole looked at Jason and shrugged. Suddenly he wanted to be done with them.

"Anything else from up there?" Jason asked.

"No, I don't think so," Klaatu said, "Not at this time. But I hope you have a clearer picture of the situation."

"Seems like something of a Hail Mary pass," Jason said, mostly to himself.

There was a look of confusion on the three faces on the screen. "It's a football term," he explained, "For when you don't have any real plan and you throw the ball towards the end zone and hope one of your people catches it."

"Ah, very good," Klaatu said. "Yes, and you are the thrower, Jason. You and Carole, and we look to Earth's best people being ready to catch the ball."

Who's Calling

After talking with heavenly beings, so to say, an earthling needs a walk on the beach to get grounded again. So it was that Carole, Jason and The Dawg found themselves plying the water's edge south of Asilomar not twenty minutes after the conversation with the above ended. They weren't all talked out, but there was something soothing about the gentle pace of the waves that induced their complementary silence for the first hundred years. Then they both spoke at the same time.

"I suppose..." Jason began.

"You were..." Carole started.

"You go," they both said together.

"Ladies first," Jason insisted.

"Jason..."

"Yes, Carole..."

"When we were talking to them, and I said something, I felt you looking at me."

"When you asked Klaatu where that left us?"

146

Carole smiled at him ever more brightly. "Yes, that was it." She paused to feel some of her heightened pleasure. "It meant so much to me. I felt your respect and your love. It wasn't like anything I'd ever felt before. Not even close."

"I never felt it either, my dear Carole. You are awesome."

They had stopped. He took her face gently into his hands and lowered his to hers. It was a kiss of moment, as he described it to her later. Their lips met and the rest of the world disappeared. At some point they returned, and recommenced their perambulation. No further comment was needed.

After a bit, Carole asked, "What were you going to say?"

"When?"

"When we talked at the same time and you said 'ladies first'."

"Ah, yes, I was going to say that I thought at some point we might sit down with a pad of paper and make notes on what messages we think might get across."

"To those who could see them."

"*Exactement.*"

"Ariane is rubbing off on you," Carole observed.

"Just the accent, my sweet," Jason laughed. "But it is a nice sounding language, isn't it?"

"*Absolument, mon cher,*" she replied.

"See what I mean?"

"Yes dear," Carole told him in her best schoolmarm. "By the way, do you think we need to translate these messages into other languages?"

"You mean because probably not every truly conscious person on our planet can speak English?"

"Yes dear."

"Ah well, if we do audio, I suppose that might be an issue, but text can be translated by Google and other programs. And ya gotta think with all those folks out there messing with everything on the Internet that someone who gets what we're saying could pick up the etymological ball and do the translating with either a voice or subtitles."

"Pick up the etymological ball," Carole repeated. "I like that. We can toss it to Klaatu and the girls when next we chat."

"Good plan," Jason said. "And by the by, I think for all the bluster, they are truly pleased that they chose us to do this."

"May that feeling last," Carole replied.

"How could it not?"

"Well, there's that, isn't there?"

"There is that, there is."

"Are we procrastinating?"

"Probably," Jason replied, "but my experience in writing has often been that I need to let my mind sit with things for a while; simmering, if you will."

"I will. I like simmering. Gives us time to talk about the ocean, The Dawg, what to make for dinner, you know."

"Yeah, the important stuff."

Jason's cellphone rang. He pulled it out of the leather holster on his belt and looked at the caller ID. "Francie L?" he read.

Carole's furrowed brow smoothed as she remembered. "Isn't that the woman we met at Cindy's party?"

"I don't remember anyone but you that night," Jason said as he opened the phone. "Hello, this is Jason," he said.

"Jason, this is Francie. Francie LeVillard. We met at Cindy Bevelaqua's house the other evening."

"Oh yes, hi."

"I don't imagine you would remember me very well," she said with a chuckle. "You seemed quite involved, as I recall."

Jason chuckled. "Quite doesn't begin to describe it," he said, "I hope I didn't seem rude."

Francie laughed. "No, not rude. Delighted, I think would be a better description."

"Yes, that sure fits."

"This is going to sound weird, but I got a call from someone named Sue Lynn or Sue Ann or something. I couldn't quite understand."

"SueLan?" Jason offered.

"That's sound like it," she agreed. "She said she knew you and asked if you and I could get together. It was important, she said, but she couldn't tell me what it was about."

"Ah."

"Ah...does that mean you know what it's about?"

"Actually, I don't but I think if we met and talked it might make sense."

"Huh, well, I'm game."

"We, too."

"We?"

"Yes, Carole Holley, the woman I was involved with at Cindy's? Well, we are more involved. And she knows SueLan, too."

"Fine with me. The more the merrier." There was doubt in her voice, but it wasn't personal. "I live south of the Carmel Highlands but I'm coming up to town in a bit. Might you, and Carole, be able to meet me in town in about an hour? Would that be convenient?"

"One sec," Jason said, and he explained the situation to Carole. She nodded her approval. "Sure. That would work. We have The Dawg with us, so perhaps, if it would work for you, we could meet at the Cypress Inn?"

"Yeah, that's fine. I like that place. Doris Day is one of the owner's I think. They have a lot of her memorabilia."

"That's the place. They also have a nice outdoor patio, with heaters if the fog is in."

"Sounds great. See you there in an hour."

"Right. Thanks," he said, closing his phone and noting the time.

"We have some strange friends," Carole observed, "and I don't mean Francie."

Jason tilted his head skyward.

"That's who I mean," Carole confirmed.

Fifty-five minutes later they were sitting at a table on the outdoor patio at the Cypress. They were about to order when Francie appeared. She smiled as she saw the couple and then The Dawg. She knelt down beside him and rubbed his head by his ears.

"You'll make a friend for life," Jason said, standing up. He shook her proffered hand. "Good to see you again."

Francie chuckled, "That's about all that happened at Cindy's. I can see why. My goodness, you two are a couple. And you just met? Amazing. Good for you."

Carole beamed and thanked her as they, too, shook hands

and Francie sat with them. About five-six with short dark hair and Basque coloring in her face, Francie was probably in her late thirties. She had a quiet presence; the kind you didn't notice unless you looked. Carole said later she had a similar feeling to Ariane Chevasse, and Jason commented that their auras were similar: conscious, purposeful, present.

When they were just getting settled, Francie's cellphone rang. She apologized when she saw who was calling and took the call. She listened and then in seconds looked shocked.

Carole was looking at Jason and saw that his head twitched slightly. Then he spoke to Francie, in a slightly distant voice. He said, "The Professor is all right. He wasn't in the explosion."

Francie's jaw dropped. She managed to say, "Hold on," to Ariane, and stared at Jason.

Jason spoke again, "There is a body in the ruins." He paused, squinted, reported, "It was a man who tried to kill him."

Francie brought the phone back to her head. "Back with you." Her eyes widen further as she listened again. "Um, not to worry. I don't want to tell you why on the phone, but not to worry. We need to meet."

She looked at Jason and pointed her finger at the table, asking if they should meet there at the Cypress.

Jason shook his head. "Not here. And later." His head twitched slightly again. "That's it," he said in his normal voice.

Francie looked at him, found the trust inside of herself and told Ariane, "I'll call you back in" -- she looked at Jason; he made a C with his fingers – "a half-hour," she said in amazement. She listened for a moment, said "Right," and disconnected the call.

She demanded in a hard tone mixed with concern, "Just what is going on? Who are you? What are you?"

"I appreciate that you went with me," he began.

"How could I not?" she asked. She turned to Carole, "Does he do this often?"

Carole smiled at Francie somewhat ruefully. "This will all make sense shortly." She looked at Jason and gave a quick laugh, then said to Francie, "This is new territory. It's marvelous that you are so grounded that you trusted him. You were right to." She looked back at Jason.

"I could hype this, but I don't think you need to be sold on anything," he looked at her and raised his eyebrows. She shook her head slowly. "First," he said, "when I told you about The Professor, I was just telling you what I was hearing. We met him yesterday so I knew his voice instantly. He was calm and strong. He was using me, I guess, to let you and then Ariane know that he was all right. That he had staged the explosion and left the body so the people who were after him might not realize what had happened for a couple of days." He paused there to give her time to object to his incredible story or to ask a question. She said nothing.

Jason took a deep breath and then provided some background. "Last week I had an experience where I thought maybe I had died, but after being in what I took as heaven, I returned to my life in the same second. While there, I was told about what I needed to do down here. It had to do with seeing auras. I was told about The Professor and his work. Tony Seton, I think you know him" – Francie nodded – "and I talked with him and he explained to me about the video he is doing on The Professor's work. And he told me that Geoffrey and Ariane were also in touch with him and The Professor." Jason paused. "While I was up there, or wherever, I met with three people or beings. One of them was a female named SueLan."

Francie narrowed her gaze at Jason, looked over at Carole and then back to Jason. "I feel like I'm an unwilling participant in a focus group," she said, "and you're trying out a new television script on me. But you're for real. I mean, this is not a scam. I guess I know that...somehow."

"Francie," Jason said earnestly, "I have never heard voices before. I heard The Professor's voice. I couldn't imagine not repeating what he said."

"That was amazing. That you knew what had happened, and that you told me about the body before Ariane said anything about it. She had just told me of the explosion."

Carole was as fascinated as Francie, even though she'd had some background with Jason and his story. "I know this sounds weird –"

Francie chuckled, "You could say that..."

Carole continued, "But it would have been even less plausible if it were only a coincidence, wouldn't it?"

That brought a brief halt to the conversation. Francie looked at Carole. "Did you die, too?" There was just the slightest trace of skepticism in her tone.

Carole smiled at her. "No, but let me tell you how we met." And she did. In concluding she said, "I don't believe in any religion, but I've always had a sense that there was some force out there, something with a purpose, and that we were all part of it. What Jason has told me, the way we got together and who we are together...I know that's not a coincidence. And it's not weird. It's everything I've ever known that I wanted."

She took advantage of Francie's silence and said, "Jason is not dead, at least not now, he's not even weird. And I can tell you his ego is healthy. This isn't about self-aggrandizement in any way. He – and now me with him – have this impossible mission..."

"Which you had no choice but to accept," Francie said with a smile on her face. She sat for a moment, nodding her head thoughtfully. "Holy Bat Cave," was all she could say and the three broke into laughter of relief.

Francie asked, "So we are directed to meet at exactly the time that Ariane would be calling me to tell me something that you were hearing in your head? No, that's not coincidence. Whew!" She shook her head, not negatively, but in amazement at what she had taken in. "So what's next?"

It was Jason's turn to shake his head. "I don't know exactly," and he looked to Carole.

"We were thinking in terms of some sort of informational marketing campaign, maybe coordinated with Tony's video release, but now I don't know." She left it there.

Jason said, "I don't know is right. I could understand that The Professor's discovery would fly in the face of certain interests." He thought a moment and then said, "You should also know what happened yesterday, while we were up in Mendocino, with Ariane and Geoffrey at The Professor's house." Then he launched into the story of finding the FBI agent on their porch when they arrived home, and what he had told them.

"Was that Mike Olsen?"

"Yes," Jason told his, his eyebrows raised.

"It's a small community," Francie explained. "Mike is one of the good guys." She was thoughtful for a long moment. "There are obviously some people who want to preserve the status quo," she said, "and at all costs."

"Apparently," said Carole. "It's good we found out before we'd put our heads on the chopping block."

Jason reached over and put her arms around Carole's neck and nuzzled against her face. "We are here for a long time, my darling Carole. Whatever the plan, we will be together for a long time. I promise."

Tears rolled down Carole's cheek. "I can't believe I lived without you for so long."

Jason kissed her and pulled away from her slowly.

Francie looked at the couple. "You sure are more than a coincidence." She took a deep breath and let it out. "So what do I tell Ariane and Geoffrey?"

Jason answered, "I wouldn't say anything yet about this conversation, if you can hold off a little bit. It might be safer for all of us if we didn't get together yet."

"Or even speak on the phone," Francie agreed. "I agree."

"At least until we know for sure what happened at The Professor's laboratory. A few days, maybe."

"Tony mentioned an organization that was tangling with The Professor, but we had no idea that this was that kind of opposition. He called it Midas Five."

The Dawg growled at her feet.

All three people looked at him. His had lifted his head but then he laid it back across his paws.

Jason nodded toward Francie, "The Dawg is also one of the good guys."

There was worry in Carole voice as she said, "Jason, I wonder if we shouldn't go home."

Jason looked at her and then at Francie. "I hope you wouldn't think us rude," he said, "but after what's happened in the past 24 hours...."

"No, certainly not," she said. "I can understand how you feel."

"Are you not concerned?" Carole asked her, surprised at her calm.

Francie gave her a light smile. "You don't know my background, and I can fill you in another time when fewer balls are in the air, as it were, but briefly, I'm a consulting detective, and I've had some experience with people who don't play by the rules. So has Ariane, if she hasn't told you, in another form. It's not to say that we shouldn't be careful, but I don't think anyone would have a reason to hurt you. Yesterday's break-in of your place was information-gathering, from what I infer from what you told me. And from Mike Olsen's reaction. He doesn't leave people hanging, and he wouldn't have been there himself if he wasn't making sure."

"That's something of a relief," Jason said. He looked over at Carole for confirmation but didn't find much. "But I'd feel better if we had both cars in the driveway and music playing."

"I completely understand," Francie said. She pulled out a business card and wrote on it. "These are my cell number and Mike Olsen's, too. Don't hesitate to call either of us, for protection or just reassurance. You are good people," she added and reached down to give The Dawg another rub. "All of you are good people."

All the Time in the World

As Carole drove them home, she asked Jason, "You don't think I'm a wuss, do you?"

"Hardly," he responded, reaching over and rubbing her shoulder. "First because I trust your instincts, and second 'cause this ain't my arena, fighting spies and such, except in my writing."

"Where it's not so real."

"Yes, like that."

"That was amazing what you did. I was watching you just before you started, what do we say, channeling?"

"I guess."

"I saw your head do a slight twitch. And then when you were done, it did it again."

"Huh. I was aware of a different feeling but I'd be hard-pressed how to describe it." Jason thought for a moment. "It wasn't bad. I guess maybe it was a little like that moving from alpha to theta waves, or whatever it is when you are falling asleep. Those few moments in between."

"Do you think it was the upstairs crowd?" Carole asked.

"Dunno," Jason answered. "It was The Professor's voice. Just like he was talking to us yesterday. He wasn't upset or anything. Just matter-of-fact. Very clear and concise, like he was relaying a message and he wanted me to hear it right."

Carole shook her head slowly.

"What?" Jason asked.

"Oh, I don't know. I was just thinking that I've never had a boyfriend like you."

Jason laughed. He brushed her cheek with his fingertips and she quickly turned her head and kissed his hand. Moments later they pulled into the driveway.

"Whaddya think, Dawg?" Jason asked as he let The Dawg out of the back seat. The Dawg looked up at the mention of his name and trotted up the walk to the front steps.

Carole came around to the front of the car and took Jason's hand. "I think he would have said something if anything were amiss."

"Yes," Jason confirmed. "Three short arfs, three long, and three more short."

"You are incorrigible," she told him as she squeezed his hand.

Jason pulled the key out of his pocket and let them into the house. All was in order downstairs, and a quick check upstairs confirmed that all was secure.

"I resent this having to feel like we've got to have this homeland security thang," he said to her waving the house key he'd used that day for the first time since he could remember.

"I know, sweetheart," Carole acknowledged, "But I have to say there really is a difference between what it felt like yesterday and how it feels today."

"Before your shower," Jason asked, trying to keep a straight face.

Carole smiled at him and sighed. "Everything's been fine since the shower," she admitted. "Except for The Professor's house blowing up with a body inside and you channeling him." She moved easily into his arms and wrapped him tightly in hers. With her head resting on his chest she asked him, "So what's next?"

"Broadway?" he offered.

"At least," she answered.

He waited until she was ready to let go of him and said, "Actually, I've been thinking."

"Really?" Carole asked. "You? Hard to believe."

"I backslide sometimes."

"So you have a plan?"

He gave her a big smile that glowed with confidence. "I do. A plan that will fulfill our obligation and get us off the hook with the folks upstairs, and also take us out of the sights of the bad guys."

"I'm all ears," Carole said gleefully. "And, I might add, not surprised at your genius."

"Why thank you, Miz Holley."

"Of course, Mr. Isaac," she responded. "Should we tell Klaatu and the others?"

"Nah, let's just do it."

"I'm for that."

"Woof," said The Dawg, looking up from his water bowl.

"It's unanimous," said Carole, laughing. She struggled to put on a serious face. "Okay, what's your plan?"

Jason explained it to her.

"That sounds very smart," she said when he was done. "I'm ready when you are."

"Okay, step one is for me to write out everything I want to say about auras and people seeing them." He headed for the stairs.

"I'll keep you supplied with cigarettes and gin," she said to him.

"I think that glass of wine we didn't have at the Cypress might lubricate the senses."

"Don't talk dirty, please. You'll never get your work done."

They laughed.

"Red or white?" she asked.

"Whatever you're pouring, my dear."

They went their separate ways, she toward the kitchen and he to his office.

Two hours later Carole heard the printer clacking and shortly after the sound had stopped, Jason came down the stairs carrying a thin sheaf of papers. He handed it to Carole with a red pen and sat down across from her. "I can't see my own typos. So if you would read it, I'll sit here quietly in case you have any questions. Okay?"

"Okay," she told him. "And you'll pour me some wine, *mon cher*?"

"*Bien sûr*," he said and popped up to go to get the bottle from the prep-island.

Here is what Jason had written.

The first thing that people must understand about auras is that they are a reflection of their true selves. A person is not his body but his soul. The body is a device to transport the soul.

The soul comes from a higher plane. You can see the footprint of the soul in images like Kirlian photography, an electroencephalogram or EEG which measures brain waves, or an electrocardiogram or EKG, which displays the heart action. There other devices, too, but those are the obvious ones.

To get a picture in your mind, think of a movie with a hospital scene where a patient is on his last legs and a monitor shows a green line that pulsates with each heartbeat. When the person dies, the line goes flat and a buzzer sounds, summoning the emergency staff. That doesn't matter.

What matters is that when the heartbeat stops registering, it means that the energy that has been keeping the body alive – the energy that is the life of the person – has departed, and all that is left is the physical presence.

That energy made the heart pump, the lungs breathe, moved all of the muscles so that they could move the body. That energy noted pain, and it repaired damaged.

That energy was also the thoughts and emotions, the ideas and the hopes and dreams and fears. It was anger and love. It was the total uniqueness of the person. It was who they were. It was their soul.

That energy arrived at the moment of conception, when the sperm and the egg got together. It is what grew the zygote into a full-fledged person.

That energy produced a personality to interface with the outside world. That energy is what we call life.

What you need to know as regards all of this and auras may already be obvious. The energy that is your life is quite visible outside the body's form. In fact, infants can see auras. It is often the reason why they react to people, positively or negatively.

But as infants become children and begin verbalizing, the very idea of seeing auras is taught out of them. Because their parents have learned not to see them since they were infants themselves, so they teach their children that they can't see them. For many children, the assertion of not seeing auras is an important part of growing up. That is why children learning from other children wind up sharing their dismissal of seeing auras.

There are some cultures where auras are prized, but few in the so-called developed world, not on a wide-scale.

The truth is that auras can be seen by anyone. It's a matter of unlearning what they have been taught and accepted.

The key to unlearning is to realize just how extraordinary being human really is. And in particular, to understand that what distinguishes us from all other species are the abilities to reflect and to imagine.

First you need to reflect on the logic of auras. Think about the fact that it is your energy that powers everything about you, both your body and your mind. Realize that this energy manifests itself every moment of your life in a million different ways that you never even think about, and much of which you take for granted, like all of the activity that keeps your body alive and well.

It's quite a system you've got working for you, this life-force energy. How your body functions is fascinating enough, but well beyond those physical mechanics is your character, which your soul energy has produced and refined to define your place in the world. It includes your dignity and integrity, courtesy and grace, your intellect, discipline, creativity, wit, and purpose. Or lack thereof. The degree of these qualities is apparent in your soul, and reflects in your aura.

So just imagine...imagine what it would be like if everyone's higher qualities were visible to everyone else. You could tell how conscious people were. You could see if they were in fear. You would know if they represented a danger. Or if they were wise and direct. It would be clear if they were present or if their minds were stuck in the past or racing into the future. You could see if they were telling the truth.

That's the power of the aura.

Just imagine what a different world this would be if we knew where everyone stood. It may sound utopian – perhaps ridiculous to some – but this would be the next stage of our evolutionary development.

It would mean peace...as a stepping stone to the potential of the best in human achievement.

It would mean intimacy with power, if that doesn't seem too abstract.

The wonder and joy of living on our Earth with such capacity and understanding is beyond the horizon of our comprehension today, but it won't be for long.

Of course many people will resist. They have been living with their limited beliefs all of their lives. They have learned from a line of similarly-minded that stretches back a hundred thousand years.

Many people – most throughout the generations – have clung to religion to get them through their troubled times, and their pleasures, but in that process, they have been externalizing the responsibility for their own lives. In simple terms, god is not outside of us. Our soul is the godhood within.

That's not going to go over well with many people certainly, but as more people expand their consciousness – and more people unblock their ability to see auras – then the tide will turn...in favor of a healthy and productive and joyous future for everyone.

It will take several generations, no doubt, and at times and in some places, the ride will have bumps in it. That's understating what we might expect. But eventually everyone will be able to see auras, and we will arrive at where we have always been headed.

Let me offer some metaphors for the transition we will be going through.

You might conjure up in your mind two images of ocean divers; one is a scuba diver swimming not far from the surface in a wetsuit, the other is a deep-sea diver in heavy, clunky diving gear with a helmet and hoses coming out of it, plodding along the ocean floor. The skin diver, with nothing between his skin and the wetsuit can swim easily. He's agile; he can turn quickly and respond immediately to what he might encounter. Whereas the guy in the heavy suit is out of direct touch with his environment. He has to manipulate the suit around him to move, to act, to deal with whatever he faces.

So it is with our own beings. That personality that the soul creates to get along in the world. If that personality is a thick mask or a shield that our soul uses to protect itself or to hide from the world, it's not so easy to function. But if that soul has made only a thin covering for itself, then he has a far more direct and immediate relationship with life around him. He's not playing games. He's not manipulating people. He's present and engaged. It's a far healthier way to live, at least in most societies, where we respect clarity and honesty more than we do an out-sized ego.

An obvious move for anyone seeking to improve their position in the world is to reduce the gap between the personality and the soul. It's a process, and it will take effort and some time, and it will almost inevitably alter your relationships. But the bottom line is that the greater congruity you have between your soul and the rest of the world, the happier, safer, and more powerful you will be because you won't have to pretend, play games, remember lies, or be someone different from who you are at your core.

You will have to be patient with yourself in this process. You will be shedding a skin, and that can leave you feeling vulnerable at times, but the fact is that the more of the personality that you shed, the stronger you are because you have less to explain and defend.

If you put yourself on this path, if you commit to the process, you will be constantly rewarded with better feelings about yourself. You will have more energy because you're not having to carry the baggage of your personality, like that weighty deep-sea diving suit. You will breathe more easily. You will feel more present. You will be more alert to the functions of your own body. And ultimately, you will be able to see the auras of everyone around you.

Here is another image that might be useful to your understanding of how your mind works. Ideas come in through the right lobe of the brain and are translated in the left lobe. (I suggest that they come from the universal consciousness, or what Jung referred to as the collective unconsciousness, but the source doesn't really matter.) The translation is mostly from the language of the source to the language of the Earth, and how those ideas fit into your terrestrial context.

Over the years of your life, the left lobe has, in most cases, added editing to its translating. That's the work of the personality who receives new ideas through a filter of its own creation. You will certainly understand this if you give some thought to how you react to news or new ideas; it is with a paradigm of pre-set, customized expectations, attitudes, fears, and hopes, et cetera. You can make wonderful progress in expanding your consciousness if you make the effort to reduce the authority of your editor in this function. The more you can let the raw ideas come through, the more value you will find in them.

There is this important truth. The more effort you apply to this process of expanding your consciousness, the bigger the results you will see, and sooner. But you always need to look inside, not outside, to gauge your progress. It's like taking off in a jet. You are racing down the runway at 180 miles an hour and the outside world is racing past you out the window. But when you have climbed to your cruising altitude and you look out the window, everything seems to be moving very slowly, even though in fact you are traveling at three times the speed you did at take off. So make the effort, but don't hurt yourself by measuring your progress by the response of others. Get your guidance from your own insides.

Understand that this is a larger challenge than changing what you think. It's about changing how you think. It's not about the inventory of your thoughts, but how you engage ideas... what you look at, what you consider or reject without considering, and how you make those choices. You have to shift your thinking habits, for they are only habits. You need to think for yourself and your soul instead of through your personality. The personality will resist; it will try to preserve its position, but step by step you can reduce the authority that you granted it, and take back the power.

In this process you will want to reduce the number of external stimuli in your life. Turn off the television. Stop listening to talk radio. Only spend time with people you respect for their character; people who act with integrity. You might try meditation. Go for long walks, alone or with someone who doesn't require a lot of conversation. Reduce the general level of "noise" around you.

Also, if it has to be said, get yourself in good physical health. No smoking, little if any alcohol, don't eat junk food, reduce your intake of sugar, caffeine and other stimulants. Shift to healthy, natural products. And get plenty of sleep. Most people really need eight hours of sleep. The healthier your body is, the better your mind will operate.

These additional observations...

– When people become more conscious, even before they can regain their sight of auras, they will always be aware from whence they came. That means they will never forget their roots, their earlier, limited consciousness. And that means they will never perpetrate violence down the ladder. All violence always rises from lower on the consciousness ladder, from people who don't know better. As you expand your consciousness, you can't imagine being violent toward someone who is less conscious. That does not mean, however, that you won't protect yourself; you have an obligation to do so.

– Most everyone has the potential for greatness; the ability to increase their consciousness beyond their current imagination. You should be aware that most people at the lower end of the social spectrum have been in a survival mode, and their first step to grow their consciousness requires that they let go of fear. The lack of security inherent in fear at the survival level can cause its own problems, and people need to be aware of that, especially the ramifications for families, clans, and tribes. The ability to read auras will enable people to recognize where there might be conflict and to avoid some of it. Very few people will listen, but here's the truth if you want to try: There is no use in being angry at the state of one's aura – yours or anyone else's. It reflects who the person really is, and it can't be faked. Increasing awareness and clearing out negative attitudes is the only thing that can do the trick.

– You will know immediately what the colors and other factors of auras mean when you see them. Their meanings are tacit in their appearance. There is no cause for worrying about reading them. Also on this point, a video is expected out shortly, if it isn't already, featuring a physicist explaining the different elements of auras and what they mean. This will be a particularly valuable tool for those people who do better when they can back up their intuitive with scientific fact.

– You might have already intuited that it is more important to focus on who you are, which generates the quality of your aura, than to spend time checking others. There was a wonderful line in one of Douglas Adams' books in which a television anchorwoman was checking herself out in the mirror by the door of her hotel room before she went down to the lobby for an important interview. And as he described the scene, "She looked cool and in charge, and if she could fool herself, she could fool anybody."

This final thought. Back in 1985, Tina Turner recorded a very powerful song entitled, *We Don't Need Another Hero*. You might hold that thought when you consider that this next, critical stage in our evolution is about personal responsibility. As we expand our consciousness, we will recognize that we don't need another hero because we must be the heros of our own time.

When Carole finished reading Jason's piece – she called it his treatise – her eyes were moist and red and she was sniffing a lot. "You've been thinking about this for more than a week, I see," she told him. "I don't suppose I have to tell you what I think, other than you looking into my face."

"You think most people will get it, what I'm saying?"

"Oh, yes, Jason." She laughed and sniffed in the same moment and the laughter won. "Anyone who doesn't get this doesn't want to. Or they're not ready for it yet. And I think a lot of people are already on the right path, with recycling, eating better, exercising, not watching horror movies, and other self-help activities."

"Will it upset a lot of people do you think?"

"Probably," she said. "There are a lot of people who will have to turn their ships around, but I think their displeasure will be focused on themselves, ultimately. If they don't go mad first. But you know, if they don't make the cut, they will come around again. That's the way it works."

"Good. That's what I wanted to accomplish."

Carole chuckled. "I so enjoy the way you complete things and are ready to move on."

"You provide that finality for me, Carole," Jason said to her softly. "You make me more efficient. What was it you said? 'One of us is great and two of us is better.'"

"Did I say that?"

"Yes ma'am, you did, and it was – it is – the truth."

"All right then, what's next?"

"I'm glad you asked," he said. "I think we should bring some food and wine – lots of food, nibbly-type stuff – to the bedroom along with a tape recorder and get our story down.

Not our life histories, but as I told you, all of the relevant details of our time together."

"I like this part of your plan. Do you have a schedule?" she asked coyly.

"I'm kinda hungry again, so we can start now and finish when we finish."

"I can see that with what you've just produced, you might want a respite," Carole said as she pulled a vegetable platter and packets of cheeses and condiments out of the refrigerator. Jason was retrieving crackers out of the cabinet and put a loaf of fresh bread into the oven to warm.

"It's funny, but when I blow something out like that, it's not the effort it must look like from the outside. It's been cooking and it was ready to serve."

Carole chuckled again. "What you produced in two hours would have ravaged any mortal man," Carole insisted. "I guess the key word is mortal."

"I think I'll open some champagne," Jason said.

Epilogue

It was Jason's plan, of course, that I write their story. He sent me his treatise, for it really was that, along with the transcripts of the recordings they made, and the recordings themselves in case I came to a place where the voice-recognition software choked on their words. Actually, the software worked quite well. Plus, my assignment was to put together a story using what they recorded, not their story verbatim, so I had plenty of latitude.

And truth be told, I had a lot of fun with it. It took me a couple of weeks because I was busy with another project that I'll tell you about in a moment. When I was done I sent the manuscript to them to error-check, and it came back to me the next day with maybe a dozen errors – what they called errors – based on my style. I asked them if they thought the "errors" were egregious or if they might not let them go so it would be in a different style that would make tracing the origins more difficult. My argument was a slam dunk.

What I was busy with was a video of The Professor that was mentioned earlier. I finished the editing and put it in a place so that it would be ready to release when it was time. I'm thinking that it will show up on the website for this book, in addition to primary locations on the web. We'll wait and see if it is in fact needed. The Professor being a humble sort won't sanction the release of the video unless the lynchpin of his strategy failed. I told him that it wouldn't hurt to have the video up anyway, since people take in information differently. He grimaced and put off making a decision.

The lynchpin was the release of a PSR phone app. It was produced and disseminated by Geoffrey and Ariane, though they kept themselves hidden by several fire walls so that no one could go after them. This freeware allows smartphone users to point their camera at anyone – or at an image or a video – and it will display the aura. There was a campaign by a political front group to discredit the software and then claim copyright infringement. That didn't do any good but generate some headlines since the PSR genie was already out of the electronic bottle, beyond the twisted arm of the law, even if they could find courts to uphold their specious claims.

Where will all this go, I couldn't even speculate. The world is in turmoil. Will Parallel Spectographic Recoloration provide stability? Not right away. But just imagine how much better life will be when we get there.

Life already got better for Carole and Jason. He received a certified letter from his landlord in Costa Rica. The man said that he wasn't coming back, and that he wanted to thank Jason for all that he had done for Apollo (The Dawg), and for his brother in Mendocino. That thanks was the enclosed transfer of title to Jason of the property where he lived, including the main house.

Yep, you guessed it. The Professor was the landlord/ surgeon's brother. Jason had no idea. It's a small world.

When Jason read the letter and held up the document, Carole woofed and The Dawg smiled.

Author

Tony Seton is a professional writer, public speaker, business and political consultant, and communications specialist. Early in his career as a broadcast journalist, he covered Watergate, six elections, and five space shots, produced Barbara Walters' news interviews, and won a handful of national awards for his business-economics coverage for ABC Network Television News. Later, he wrote and produced two award-winning public television documentaries. He has conducted over a thousand interviews and is the author of more than 2,000 essays and a dozen books.

As a political consultant, Tony's clients have included Nancy Pelosi and Tom Campbell. Other hats he's worn include teacher, media trainer, and web designer.

When he's not working, Tony is flying, taking photographs, and walking on the beach....though even then he's often communicating, with other denizens of the dunes, both human and avian.

Other Books from Tony Seton

My principal activity over the past year or so has been the writing, editing, and publishing of books. A half-dozen in the past year. They include fiction and non-fiction and a new hybrid I call non-non-fiction. These are based on real events and/or circumstances and are designed to engage the reader and – he said humbly – to move us all forward in our thinking. Among the recent titles are

MAYHEM is a contemporary novel set in Marin County, California based on the mythic struggle between good and evil, with the author being called in to tip the tide of the titanic battle.

THE AUTOBIOGRAPHY OF JOHN DOUGH, GIGOLO is a novel about a former hedge fund manager who decides on a new path – to improve the lives of women. His clients include widows, divorcees and a gangster's moll.

SILVER LINING is a novel about a shooting on the street that brings reporter David Skye and nurse Lucy Balfour together, for what becomes excitement and romance

THE OMEGA CRYSTAL is a page-turner of a novel about how the petro industry is sitting on crucial developments in solar power capture and storage, waiting until their inventories run dry. Anchorman Geoff Lance uncovers the truth with the help – and love from – Ariane Chevasse, the beautiful and brilliant daughter of the inventor of The Omega Crystal.

TRUTH BE TOLD is a novelized version of a true story about an historic civil rights case of sexual harassment against a top-50 American law school.

FROM TERROR TO TRIUMPH / THE HERMA SMITH CURTIS STORY A true story of a young girl's survival of the Nazi occupation of Austria and her creation of a successful new life on the Monterey Peninsula.

VISION FOR A HEALTHY CALIFORNIA is a road map for the Golden State. Written by Bill Monning, the highly-esteemed member of the California Assembly.

THREE LIVES OF A WARRIOR is the stunning memoir of Phil Butler, who spent eight years as a prisoner of the North Vietnamese and came home to a new life.

THE POWER OF THE I AM by Dan Shafer is a breakthrough in self-awareness, and puts the power of meditation within reach of millions of people.

If you are interested in these books, or in having your own book written, edited and or published, please go online to

TonySeton.com

We always welcome your comments.

Made in the USA
Charleston, SC
28 November 2011